Praise for Vicki Lewis Thompson

"Thompson continues to do what she does best, tying together strong family values bound by blood and choice, interspersed with the more sizzling aspects of the relationship."
—*RT Book Reviews* on *Thunderstruck*

"Intensely romantic and hot enough to singe... her Sons of Chance series never fails to leave me worked up from all the heat, and then sighing with pleasure at the happy endings!"
—*We Read Romance* on *Riding High*

"Vicki Lewis Thompson has compiled a tale of this terrific family, along with their friends and employees, to keep you glued to the page and ending with that warm and loving feeling."
—*Fresh Fiction* on *Cowboys and Angels*

"If I had to use one word to describe *Ambushed!* it would be *charming*... Where the story shines and how it is elevated above others is the humor that is woven throughout."
—*Dear Author*

"The chemistry between Molly and Ben is off the charts: their first kiss is one of the best I've ever read, and the sex is blistering and yet respectful, tender and loving."
—*Fresh Fiction* on *A Last Chance Christmas*

"*Cowboy Up* is a sexy joy ride, balanced with good-natured humor and Thompson's keen eye for detail. Another sizzling romance from the RT Reviewers' Choice award winner for best Blaze."
—*RT Book Reviews*

Dear Reader,

Can you think of a better time to fall in love than Christmas? What could be more romantic than sparkling lights and glowing candles? Plus, if you're lucky enough to live in cowboy country, winter prompts the guys to break out those sheepskin coats that make their shoulders look a mile wide. When they turn the collar up and tug the Stetson down against a cold wind, what's not to love?

My Christmas present to you this year is Ty Slater, who happens to own both a sheepskin coat and a Stetson. You're welcome. Ty can't wait for Christmas to arrive. After the holidays the promotional calendar for his foster parents' new project at Thunder Mountain Ranch flips over to January, and he will no longer be the shirtless cowboy who's decorated walls all over Wyoming since September. But Whitney Jones, who's been crushing on Ty's calendar shot for weeks, isn't nearly so eager to turn the page. Maybe she'll have to make do with Ty himself!

I'm thrilled to welcome you back to Thunder Mountain for the holidays. Everyone's missed you! Rosie and Herb are looking forward to a festive season now that the financial crisis that threatened their ranch this summer is over. Even better, Cade and Damon are back to stay, and Ty's come home for a visit. Thanks to Damon's skill with a staple gun, multicolored lights are strung along the roofline. Cade just finished plowing the road so you won't need four-wheel drive to make it up to the house. Come spend Christmas with the Thunder Mountain Brotherhood!

Festively yours,

Vicki Lewis Thompson

Vicki Lewis Thompson

A Cowboy Under the Mistletoe

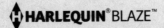

Recycling programs
for this product may
not exist in your area.

ISBN-13: 978-0-373-79875-9

A Cowboy Under the Mistletoe

Copyright © 2015 by Vicki Lewis Thompson

Printed in U.S.A.

A passion for travel has taken *New York Times* bestselling author **Vicki Lewis Thompson** to Europe, Great Britain, the Greek isles, Australia and New Zealand. She's visited most of North America and has her eye on South America's rain forests. Africa, India and China beckon. But her first love is her home state of Arizona, with its deserts, mountains, sunsets and—last but not least—cowboys! The wide-open spaces and heroes on horseback influence everything she writes. Connect with her at vickilewisthompson.com, facebook.com/vickilewisthompson and twitter.com/vickilthompson.

Books by Vicki Lewis Thompson

Harlequin Blaze

Thunder Mountain Brotherhood
Midnight Thunder
Thunderstruck
Rolling Like Thunder

Sons of Chance
Lead Me Home
Feels Like Home
I Cross My Heart
Wild at Heart
The Heart Won't Lie
Cowboys & Angels
Riding High
Riding Hard
Riding Home
A Last Chance Christmas

To get the inside scoop on Harlequin Blaze and its talented writers, be sure to check out BlazeAuthors.com.

All backlist available in ebook format.

Visit the author profile page at Harlequin.com for more titles.

For my mom, Randy Shutt, who taught me everything I know about making Christmas special.

1

Ty Slater was beat, but the decorated streetlamps in Sheridan's historic business district perked him up considerably. A large dose of caffeine would help even more. He parked in front of Rangeland Roasters, a family-owned coffee shop that had originated in Cheyenne but had recently expanded to a second location in Sheridan.

They brewed great coffee, and he'd meant to check out the new shop when he'd visited his foster parents back in August. So he'd try it out now, instead. He didn't want to arrive at Thunder Mountain Ranch for Thanksgiving weekend dragging ass. If he did, Rosie and Herb would fuss over him.

Years ago he wouldn't have minded a little fussing. But he was twenty-seven for God's sake, with a grown-up job as a contract lawyer at a well-respected Cheyenne firm.

He'd burned the midnight oil to get his work done before the holiday, and a cup of coffee would keep him from falling asleep during the pre-Thanksgiving Day supper, which was guaranteed to feature tuna casserole. He loved that casserole almost more than he loved the turkey dinner they'd enjoy tomorrow.

He climbed out of his truck into slushy snow that had gathered near the curb. Gray clouds promised more of the same before nightfall, which made the cozy coffee shop even more inviting. Candy canes and delicate snowflake decorations covered the windows, and an evergreen wreath topped with a red bow hung on the door.

Stomping the slush from his boots, he stepped inside where warmth and the fragrance of roasted coffee beans and peppermint greeted him. Manly cowboy types weren't supposed to like flavored coffee, but he might break ranks and order the one they called Peppermint Pleasure.

He unbuttoned his shearling coat and glanced around. The place had drawn a crowd on this cold November afternoon, so most of the tables were taken. A Christmas tree in the corner decorated with coffee-related ornaments looked similar to the tree he'd seen in the Cheyenne location. The tree topper featured the Rangeland Roasters logo, a double *R* positioned back-to-back on a tan coffee mug.

Branding was always a good thing, and this shop felt very much like the one in Cheyenne. A cheerful buzz of conversation overlaid the carols playing in the background. Fortunately for the owners, the expansion gamble appeared to have paid off.

As he stood in line waiting to order, he recognized one of the baristas who used to work in the Cheyenne location. She'd made an impression on him last summer with her jaunty blond ponytail and ready smile. She was at least five-ten and looked athletic, as if she might be a runner and possibly a skier.

He pictured the nametag she'd worn in Cheyenne. Whitney. An unusual name, but he would have remembered it anyway. When something was important to him, he took a mental snapshot and stored it away.

He'd felt the tug of mutual attraction whenever she'd taken his order but he'd been dating someone during the time she'd worked in Cheyenne. She might have been involved with somebody, too. He hadn't bothered to find out because there'd been no point.

Then one day she wasn't there anymore and he hadn't asked about that, either. Now she'd popped back into his life and he was ridiculously happy to see her. He should ignore that sudden burst of pleasure.

He wasn't dating anyone these days, but getting involved with a woman who lived in Sheridan made no sense. As many hours as he put in at the firm, being separated by a five-hour drive wasn't an optimal situation. And that was assuming she was free and he'd been right about her interest.

All that aside, he looked forward to saying hello and finding out how things were going. The dynamic with the other two employees suggested she was in charge, so maybe she'd been given the manager's job. He wouldn't be surprised considering her brisk efficiency and easy rapport with customers.

Then he saw the calendar on the wall behind her. Aw, hell, he'd forgotten. He'd probably find it plastered all over town. He pulled his Stetson a little lower over his eyes. Like that would help.

There he was in all his glory—shirtless, arms folded on the rail of a corral, hat at a rakish angle and a cocky grin on his unshaven mug. The photographer had insisted on the scruff. The other guys had been clean-shaven and she'd wanted him to look as if he'd just crawled out of bed with a lover.

Apparently he did look like that. He'd had several

women hit on him as a result of the calendar and he'd had a brief affair with one of them. She'd expected him to live up to that manufactured image and hadn't been the least bit interested in getting to know who he really was. After that he'd turned down any similar invitations.

He had no one to blame but himself. He'd been the genius who'd suggested a beefcake calendar to promote Thunder Mountain Academy, a new project based at the ranch where he'd lived as a foster kid for three years. The residential school for older teens was designed to teach them everything about horses, plus bring in some much-needed revenue. Turned out his foster parents had been the victims of a Ponzi scheme that had sucked up their life savings.

Ty had been willing to help the cause, and his legal training had come in handy for the Kickstarter campaign that had raised the startup funds for the academy. Because the calendar had been his idea, he'd been talked into being the first pinup guy. He hadn't factored in that a sixteen-month calendar meant he'd be decorating walls everywhere from September through December. He couldn't wait for January first.

He'd taken his share of ribbing from the other lawyers in the firm. The guys thought he should be thrilled that he'd attracted so much female attention. Most of the women in the office now looked at him with a gleam in their eye, even the married ladies. It was embarrassing.

He should be over it by now. He should be used to walking into a public place and seeing himself hanging on the wall. He wasn't.

He looked away from the calendar and met Whitney's brown gaze. "Hi, there, Whitney! Great to see you again. How's it going?" Maybe she'd just ignore the calendar issue.

"Good, real good." She grinned and tilted her head toward the calendar. "And here I thought you were a straightlaced lawyer type."

So she wasn't going to ignore it. Well, he couldn't blame her. He was on a beefcake calendar and most people found that intriguing, especially if they'd only known him as a white-collar professional. "I'm extremely straightlaced. And anal. You should see my sock drawer."

"Sounds like fun."

"Trust me, it's not." Damn it all, each and every time this happened he felt vulnerable, and not only because he was half naked in the picture. Anyone who read the accompanying text would learn he'd been a foster boy at Thunder Mountain Ranch. He wasn't ashamed of it, not at all, but still…the information was personal.

He hadn't figured on that kind of exposure when he'd agreed to be the first poster boy for the academy. He'd been swept up in the emotional campaign to save Thunder Mountain Ranch so Rosie and Herb could live out their golden years there. They deserved that.

They'd been put in dire straits through no fault of their own, sort of like he'd been when his parents had died. He'd wanted to help make things right for them. He still did, but man, the calendar stint had been more than he'd bargained for.

Whitney's expression softened. "Sorry to tease you about it. You're probably sick of people doing that."

"It's okay. It's for a good cause."

"Absolutely. So what can I get for you? As I recall, you like black coffee, no embellishments."

"Usually that's true." So she'd remembered his coffee order. Flattering. And he hadn't imagined that tug of mutual attraction last summer, either. They liked each other. Even better, she'd liked him before the calendar had appeared.

He glanced behind him to see if he was holding up the line. Apparently he was at the end of it. "But today I want one of those Peppermint Pleasure lattes, instead."

"Festive choice. Whipped cream?"

"No thanks. Don't want to get too wild and crazy."

"Your choice, but the whipped cream really makes it sing. We sprinkle candy cane chips on top to give the whipped cream some crunch."

"Do you like it like that?"

She held his gaze. "Love it."

Well, now. He suspected they'd moved beyond the subject of peppermint lattes. The room suddenly grew warmer. "Then I guess you'd better lather on the whipped cream and candy cane chips."

"Good decision. For here or to go?"

"I'll drink it here."

The dark-haired girl standing beside Whitney picked up a cup. "So that's a large Peppermint—"

"That's okay, Meryl. I've got this." Whitney neatly plucked the cup out of her hand. "Have a seat wherever you can find a space, Ty. I'll bring it to you."

"Thanks, but I haven't paid yet."

"Oh, right." Her laugh was slightly breathless. "Meryl, can you please handle that for me?"

"Absolutely." Meryl stepped to the cash register and took the bill he handed her. "So you're really the guy on that calendar?"

"'Fraid so."

"You should be proud of it. That's an awesome picture, and the calendar's for a great cause. I'd love to attend that academy, but I'm too old. I just turned twenty."

"Maybe eventually they'll open it up to adults." He

pocketed his change and added money to the tip jar. "You're not the only one who's expressed an interest. Maybe I should mention it while I'm at the ranch this weekend."

"I wish you would. Sounds great for kids trying to figure out what they want to do with their lives. But if you could add a special session for those of us who are still trying to figure that out but don't qualify, agewise, I'll bet you'd get some takers."

"Okay, I'll ask."

"Thanks. And you're even cuter in person." Then she blushed. "Did I just say that out loud?"

He smiled. What a sweetheart. "It's okay."

"At least you're not all stuck-up about being on the calendar. Some guys would be."

"Yeah, definitely," said the other girl, who'd been filling the napkin dispenser and the cream pitcher. She looked to be about the same age as Meryl. She stared at him with an adoring expression. "They'd be all *I'm so hot.*"

"Not my style." Another customer came up behind him and he moved out of the way. "Guess I'd better find a seat." He quickly located an unoccupied table.

So this was the effect of media on a guy's rep. Multiply this by a hundred different sexy impressions, and no wonder movie stars were mobbed. The photographer had created an image of him that didn't exist, and yet women bought into it.

He didn't roll out of bed and pull on jeans, boots and a hat before going out to take care of the horses. He hadn't even done that when he'd lived at Thunder Mountain. Guys might have tackled the morning chores before shaving, assuming they'd had enough of a beard to worry about, but they'd always put on a shirt.

Okay, maybe a few times he'd repaired a fence or shoveled manure without a shirt on. When the job was especially hot and dirty, a cowboy might go bare-chested. But it was the exception to the rule.

Whitney brought over his latte topped with an expert swirl of whipped cream and lightly sprinkled with candy cane bits. "Now isn't that pretty?"

"Sure is." He lifted the cup. Cool, soft whipped cream tickled his upper lip as he got a mouthful of…paradise. Coffee, steamed milk and peppermint was a drink fit for the gods.

Licking away the whipped cream, he swept up a few crunchy pieces of candy cane. He closed his eyes and sighed. "Oh, yeah."

"See what you've been missing?"

"Yep." And he wasn't talking about the latte. He looked up at her standing beside his table in her tan Rangeland Roasters shirt and a matching skirt that swished around her knees when she walked. In Cheyenne she'd worn slacks like everyone else. Maybe the skirt was another indication that she was the boss around here.

He decided to seize the day and worry about complications later. "Listen, I'm here until Sunday. Is there any time we might get together for…" He paused in confusion. His first move was always a coffee date but Whitney worked in a coffee shop.

She laughed softly. "Coffee?"

"No, I guess not. A different kind of drink, something involving alcohol." He hesitated. "Unless you're seeing someone?"

She shook her head. "Nope."

"Good." Adrenaline rushed through his system, or maybe it was the caffeine. Either way, his heart beat faster.

"I take it you're not with Theresa anymore?"

He blinked in surprise. "You know her?"

"Only by the name I wrote on her coffee cup whenever you'd come in together."

"Good memory. And no, I'm not with Theresa." He met her gaze. "If I had been, I wouldn't have asked you out."

"I figured, but it never hurts to be sure."

"Absolutely." He liked her direct approach. "So what's your schedule? I'm tied up tomorrow, but after that I'm flexible."

"Tomorrow wouldn't work for me, either. I'm covering for several of my employees so they can spend Thanksgiving with their families."

"Then you *are* the manager."

"Yeah, it was a terrific opportunity and I grabbed it."

"Good for you. But I guess you might not be able to take much time off, considering it's a holiday weekend." He couldn't believe how disappointed he was.

"I will be pretty busy, but I scheduled some free time Friday night to decorate my tree. Want to help me?"

"Sure!" His world brightened. "Can I bring takeout for dinner?"

"That would be wonderful. I don't know if you like Chinese, but—"

"I do. Any special requests?"

"I like almost anything, so you can surprise me."

"All right." He couldn't remember ever making a date so effortlessly.

"I get off at six, so give me a half hour to change clothes and haul out the decorations. Got your phone?"

He pulled it out of his coat pocket and keyed in her number and her address as she gave it to him. "And your last name is?"

"Jones. You can text me your number so I have it in case there's a problem with staffing Friday night, but I don't expect one."

"Doing that right now. And by the way, my last name's Slater."

"I know. It's on the calendar."

"Oh." He glanced up from his phone. "Right."

"I've only known you as Ty, but would you rather be called Tyrone?"

"Tyrone's for my clients. Ty's for my friends."

"I doubt I'll ever be your client." She smiled. "So I'll see you Friday night."

"You will, and I'll be armed with Chinese food." He hesitated, almost afraid to say anything more in case he was reading too much into this invitation to help with her tree. "It'll be nice to get to know each other better."

Awareness flashed in her brown eyes. "I think so, too."

2

THE UNEXPECTED APPEARANCE of Ty Slater helped Whitney get through the next day without feeling too sorry for herself. She'd never spent Thanksgiving away from her family and she missed that rowdy, irreverent bunch. Nearly everyone on both her mom's and her dad's side lived in Cheyenne, including all four grandparents and the majority of her aunts, uncles and cousins.

Hosting Thanksgiving rotated among those who had the space and extra chairs, and the routine hadn't varied for as long as she could remember. The midday meal was followed by touch football for those who enjoyed it and bowl games on TV for everyone else. She looked forward to that touch football game all year, but today someone else would have to take her position as wide receiver.

Sometimes her shift at Rangeland Roasters had kept her from participating in everything, but she'd made do with leftovers, the annual Ping-Pong tournament and endless games of Yahtzee. Even when she'd had to work on Thanksgiving, she'd never lost out entirely on the fun and the food. Until today.

To cheer herself up, she focused on her Friday night tree-trimming date with Ty. Looking at his picture on the calendar had been giving her a thrill for weeks, but now it provided an extra shot of adrenaline. They were going to hang out for the evening. She could barely believe her good luck.

She'd had a crush ever since he'd shown up at the coffee shop about a year ago. No surprise that he'd had a girlfriend, considering those knowing gray eyes and easy smile. He'd made her heart flutter again today, especially when he'd told her the girlfriend was history.

After reading his short bio on the calendar, she'd wondered if he might walk into this shop eventually. And so he had, looking more like a cowboy than the lawyer she'd known in Cheyenne. Discovering his hidden depths had been a turn-on, but seeing him shirtless had been a total game changer. Tyrone Slater was beautiful.

But he was uncomfortable with the calendar picture, which made him all the more adorable. She'd noticed him pull his hat lower when he'd seen it hanging on the back wall. That one gesture had been enough to make her melt.

The hat ramped up his sexy quotient, even if it covered up his glossy hair. She always noticed hair, and at first glance his had seemed to be French roast brown. But a closer look had revealed some dark red that reminded her of espresso in a glass mug held up to the light.

Back then he'd been out of reach. No longer, though. At least for this weekend, he was quite reachable.

She wouldn't have missed the opportunity to manage the new location, but if she still lived in Cheyenne... No use dwelling on that inconvenience. He probably drove up to Sheridan often to visit his foster parents at Thunder Mountain Ranch. And maybe none of that would matter because their Friday night date could be a bust.

No, it wouldn't. She'd seen the light in his eyes. He

was looking forward to the evening as much as she was. They'd clicked from their first conversation on opposite sides of the coffee shop counter. But he'd had a girl-friend then.

For whatever reason, though, Theresa was out of the picture and Theresa's loss was Whitney's gain. Timing was everything, and meeting Ty yesterday felt like the hand of Fate. Those thoughts sustained her through most of Thanksgiving Day, but around five, when the touch football game was probably over, she gave in to a fresh wave of homesickness. Ducking into her small office, she pulled out her phone.

Her mom answered immediately. "Finally! I was so afraid you'd be too busy to call. We all miss you so much!"

Whitney swallowed a sudden lump in her throat. "I miss you, too, but it was either Thanksgiving or Christmas. I couldn't justify leaving on both holidays."

"I understand. We all do. But I wish you could have heard your young cousins rave about your legendary skill at touch football. You would have felt like a first-draft pick in the NFL."

"Maybe by next year I'll have an assistant I can trust to handle Thanksgiving here."

"Maybe." Her mother paused. "But honey, if Sheridan is where you're supposed to end up, that's not so bad. It's not like the far side of the moon."

"It feels a little bit that way right now."

"I know, but this is your first Thanksgiving away from home. It'll get easier."

Whitney chuckled softly. "Are you trying to convince me or you?"

"Probably me. I knew you'd leave a big hole, but it's a little bigger than I anticipated."

It was a rare admission of vulnerability and Whitney sucked in a breath. "Aw, Mom, I'm sorry. This seemed like a good idea at the time, but maybe—"

"Don't you dare consider giving it up, Whitney Lenore! It's a terrific opportunity, and I'll adjust. You'll adjust. We'll be fine, and stronger for the experience. Buck up, sweetheart. And so will I. Christmas is less than a month away."

"Yeah, it is. That's not long."

"Not long at all. Do you have a tree for your apartment? That's very important. Yes, you'll be here for the actual day, but you need your own tree."

"I do. In fact…" She hesitated. She hadn't had the best of luck with guys and her mom worried. "Do you remember the lawyer I mentioned, the one who's on the calendar you saw when you came up here in October?"

"I certainly do! That was a memorable picture."

"He came into Rangeland Roasters yesterday and asked me out."

"Oh, my. Are you going?"

"Sort of. I invited him to help me decorate my tree tomorrow night. He's bringing Chinese."

"Oh." The silence on the other end was filled with her mother's unspoken thoughts. "That calendar picture makes him look…"

"I know, but he's not really like that. He's actually very sweet."

"He doesn't look sweet."

In her heart of hearts, Whitney hoped he wasn't, either. She was ready for the sexual adventure promised by Ty's rakish expression in the photo. But that wasn't something she was about to admit to her mother. "Take my word for it. He is. He's embarrassed by that picture."

"If you say so. At least you know something of his

background. I admire anyone who's pulled himself up by his bootstraps."

"And it's not as if he's a stranger. He patronized the Cheyenne location for months while I was still there. We talked a lot."

"But he didn't ask you out?"

"He was dating someone else."

More silence. "I'm sure he's a very nice young man."

"He is." Whitney could almost hear her mother's questions. She wanted to know if Ty changed girlfriends as easily as he changed razor blades. She wanted to know if Ty understood that her daughter was an amazing woman not to be trifled with.

Whitney had no definitive answers for those questions. Her instincts told her that she could trust Ty, but she had no hard evidence to support her belief. And she'd been wrong before. Her mother had been there to pick up the pieces, so she could be forgiven for being suspicious, especially when her precious child was five hours away.

"He'd better treat you well," her mother said at last, "or he'll answer to me."

"Thanks, Mom." Even at twenty-six, she treasured the protective tone in her mother's voice. "If he gets out of line, I'll tell him that."

"Be sure that you do. And now your cousins are dying to tell you about the disastrous football game. Do you have a few more minutes?"

"You bet."

"Then I'll walk into the living room and put you on speaker so everyone can talk. Is that okay?"

"That's more than okay. And Mom?"

"What, honey?"

"I love you."

"I love you, too, sweetheart." There was a telltale catch in her mother's voice. "So here's the group."

WITH NINE PEOPLE sitting down for Thanksgiving, Ty's foster mother, Rosie, had moved the festivities to the rec room. A wooden cover turned the pool table into a dining table. Although the original tablecloth had worn out, she'd used the same red-and-white-checked material for the new one. Tradition was important to Rosie.

She was in her element on a day like this, surrounded by friends and family. She'd had her hair freshly cut and colored its usual blond, although she'd added some sassy red streaks. Herb looked fit and his gaze was clear and untroubled. Ty loved seeing his foster parents happy and relaxed after the drama of almost losing the ranch.

Yet the crisis had turned out to be a blessing in disguise. It had brought Cade Gallagher and Damon Harrison, the first two boys Rosie and Herb had fostered, back home. Then Cade had reunited with his high school sweetheart, Lexi Simmons.

Rosie had to be thrilled about that. Lexi was like a daughter to her and Lexi's parents were dear friends. Judging from the dinner table banter between Cade and the people who could turn out to be his in-laws, Janine and Aaron Simmons had forgiven him for breaking their daughter's heart five years ago.

Like most of the boys at the ranch, Ty had once had a huge crush on Lexi. Petite and curvy, with wavy brown hair and hazel eyes that sparkled most of the time, she'd been a welcome sight whenever she'd come out to visit, either alone or with her folks. But after she'd hooked up with Cade, all the guys had backed off, especially Damon, who was probably Cade's best friend in the world.

For years Damon had acted as if he'd never settle down, but now he'd apparently found the perfect partner in Philomena Turner, a feisty redhead. Or rather Rosie had found him the perfect partner. It was obvious to anyone who knew Rosie that she'd deliberately thrown those two together last July. She wanted her boys to find true love and she was always willing to lend a helping hand whether they wanted her to or not.

Ty had been thinking about that. Living in Cheyenne had kept him a safe distance from Rosie's machinations, but yesterday he'd made a date here in Sheridan right under her nose. He wouldn't attempt to keep it a secret, either.

Yeah, like he could. Sheridan was a small town and even though Whitney was new here, chances were good that Rosie had met her. Rangeland Roasters must have contributed to the Kickstarter campaign or they wouldn't have the calendar hanging on the wall.

"Who's up for some boot scootin' tomorrow night?" Cade glanced around the table laden with the remains of their feast. "Lexi and I thought we'd check out the new band."

"I'm game." Damon pushed back his chair. "That'll give me twenty-four hours to recover. At the moment I can barely move, let alone do the two-step." He turned to Phil. "Are you willing to have me steer you around the floor tomorrow night?"

"I'm willing, but you'd better wear your steel-toed boots. I haven't danced since August and I doubt I've improved since then."

"I can't remember the last time Rosie and I danced," Herb said. "How about it, Rosie? Think we can keep up with these kids?"

"Ha." Rosie grinned. "They'll have to keep up with

us. Janine, you and Aaron should go, too. We'll show them how it's done."

"I claim a dance with Ty." Lexi smiled at him and ignored Cade's eye-roll. "I remember how you cleared the floor at prom doing all that fancy stuff with Nancy Bennett."

"Nancy's married with a baby on the way." Rosie looked at Ty and shrugged. "But that's okay. She was a good dancer but she wasn't right for you."

"Then I guess we have a plan." Cade pushed back his chair, too. "Let's take care of the dishes and then rack up the balls. I feel a pool tournament coming on."

"I won't be able to make it tomorrow night." Ty figured that would be a conversation stopper, and sure enough, everyone sat back down and turned to stare at him.

Rosie frowned. "Please tell me you're not driving back to Cheyenne so you can work the rest of the weekend"

"No, I'm not. I… I have a date."

"Oh." Rosie's frown transformed into a smile. "How nice."

"So bring her," Cade said.

"Yeah, you should." Lexi studied him with obvious interest. "Anybody we know?"

"Probably. She's the manager at Rangeland Roasters."

"Oh, *Whitney.*" Rosie said her name as if announcing the new Miss America. "What a sweetheart. She's the one who talked her boss into contributing to our Kickstarter campaign. Now I get it. You probably know her from the Cheyenne location."

"Yep."

"Did you date when she was down there?"

"No, but—"

"Doesn't matter." Rosie waved a hand in the air.

"You've reconnected with her, and that's the important thing. I can see you and Whitney together. Hadn't thought about it before, but I'll bet you two will get along like a house afire."

"I can see that," Lexi said. "I like Whitney a lot. Very personable."

"Yeah, she's great," Phil added. "Damon and I go in for coffee all the time and she's always friendly."

Ty shifted in his chair. "Look, it's just a date. No big expectations."

"Does she like to dance?" Damon had been watching the proceedings with a little smile, as if he enjoyed having someone else take the heat for a change.

"I don't know, but she's set aside tomorrow night to decorate her tree and she asked if I'd help. I'm bringing Chinese." He probably shouldn't have added the last part. Better not to offer extra details.

"Cozy." Rosie's blue eyes lit with excitement.

"Casual." Ty should have lied and said they were going to the movies, except he had no idea what was showing. Besides, no one ever got away with lying to Rosie. She could spot a fib at twenty paces.

"Well, you know where we'll be," Lexi said. "If you finish up and want to head over and join us, tell her we'd love that. I think she'd fit right in."

"She definitely would." Rosie was beaming. "You should have seen her face light up when I brought in the calendar."

"Oh, *yeah*." Cade leaned forward and gave Ty a wicked-ass grin. "I forgot all about that. She's been staring at your manly chest for months, hasn't she? Nice job. Way to work it."

"That—" He caught himself before he said *damn calendar*. "It had nothing to do with anything." Which wasn't quite true. Whitney had looked at him differently yesterday. She'd toned down her reaction after she'd realized he wanted her to let it go, but the calendar had been a factor.

"Leave the poor guy alone," Lexi said. "He's been a good sport about his extended run."

"Good point, Lex." Cade attempted to look apologetic but it didn't quite work. "You took one for the team, bro, and we all appreciate it." Then his grin reappeared. "But you have to admit it's turning out quite nicely."

3

WHITNEY HAD GIVEN herself very little time to get ready, which was just as well. All day she'd been telling herself this date was no big deal. But as she quickly changed out of her uniform into jeans and a white cable-knit sweater, she admitted to being nervous. Her heart raced every time she thought about Ty appearing outside her door.

She'd straightened her small apartment before leaving for work and she'd pulled out the box of tree ornaments. The fragrant Scotch pine she'd bought early this morning was medium-sized, a little over six feet, but that was plenty big enough for her living room. It looked great tucked in the corner.

A futon doubled as a couch because she'd wanted extra sleeping space when her friends or her folks visited. Besides the futon, the living room furniture included two end tables, two lamps and a bookcase that held her TV. Oh, and the rocker from her mother, who believed every home should have one.

Other than that, she owned a small kitchen table and matching chairs, a queen-sized bed and a dresser. Decorating wasn't her thing and she was grateful that Rangeland Roasters had a template for each holiday. Her boss

Ginny shipped the materials and Whitney let her staff go crazy.

The one exception to her lack of interest in decorating was her Christmas tree. Her mom had faithfully bought dated ornaments every year since Whitney and Selena had been born. Selena's sixteen ornaments were packed away in her parents' basement, but Whitney had all twenty-seven of hers, including the newest one her mother had mailed last week.

Whitney's box of decorations included two strands of lights plus the glass icicles and snowflakes she'd added a couple of years ago. She used wired red-and-gold ribbon instead of a garland and was still debating her options for a tree topper. Her parents had a lovely star, but she favored angels. She hadn't found one she liked, so for now she used a small teddy bear she'd had since she was four.

Five minutes before Ty was due to arrive, she thought about what they'd drink with their Chinese food. A good hostess would have a couple of bottles of wine available, or a six-pack of beer. What if he liked soda? She didn't have any of that, either. Mostly she had…coffee.

Apparently she'd stumbled into the right profession because she loved coffee—caffeinated, decaffeinated and flavored. She had an espresso machine and a professional-grade blender that could mix up an iced coffee drink that would melt in your mouth.

She knew Ty liked coffee, but it didn't seem like the right choice for Chinese food. What, then? Well, she sometimes drank tea when she ate at a Chinese restaurant, but mostly she considered it a weak version of coffee and not worth the bother. Consequently she didn't stock it at home.

About the time she'd decided water was her only

option, her intercom buzzed. Showtime. Anticipation jacked up her pulse rate as she walked to the intercom and opened the connection. "Ty?"

"Yep."

The sound of his deep baritone made her quiver. "Come on up. Second floor, number two-oh-four."

"Got it."

A manly voice for a manly man. She buzzed him in before opening her apartment door and stepping into the hall. His boots sounded on the stairs and then he came down the hallway toward her. He held a bulging plastic bag in one hand and a bottle of wine in the other.

But she was more interested in the man than what he'd brought for dinner. He wore his shearling coat, snug jeans and a brown Stetson dampened by melting snow. She couldn't remember opening her door to a more appealing sight.

His gray gaze warmed as it met hers. "I've never seen you dressed in anything but a Rangeland Roasters uniform. You look different."

"That uniform isn't exactly the height of fashion."

"No, but…you do it justice."

"Thanks." She tingled with awareness. If she'd imagined this might be a platonic evening spent in casual conversation, he'd just changed the game. Then again, she'd never believed their date would be casual and platonic.

She stepped back from the door. "Come in. And thanks for bringing wine. I had no idea what we'd drink with dinner."

"Tea is traditional, but I wasn't in the mood for tea." He brought the chill of a cold Wyoming night with him as he walked in, along with the exotic scents of Asian spices, a whiff of pine-scented aftershave and a crackle of electricity.

She hadn't realized how he filled a space until he stood in her living room. She'd hosted a couple of her girlfriends since she'd moved here, and her folks had visited twice, but the apartment hadn't felt truly small until Ty Slater stepped inside. She wasn't complaining. He was the most exciting guest she'd ever had.

"Nice tree. Smells great."

"Doesn't it? That's Christmas to me."

"Agreed." His smile flashed. "It isn't Christmas until there's a tree in the living room. How do you want to do this? We could eat while decorating, or eat first and then decorate, or vice versa. Your call."

"I'm starving and we don't want the food to get cold, so let's eat first."

"Works for me." He lifted the plastic bag and the wine bottle. "Where to?"

"All I have is the kitchen table."

"Hey, that's all I have, too. My apartment is about the size of yours. In fact, I have that same futon. Did you get yours in Cheyenne?"

"Uh-huh." She led the way into her tiny kitchen. "From that furniture store that's always running sales."

"That's the one." He set the bag and wine on her small round table.

"Did your salesman have a Santa Claus beard?"

"Yep, same guy." He took off his coat and hung it over the back of one of the chairs. The movement stirred up the scent of whatever soap he'd used, something lemony.

Whitney took a deep breath. Having this man around was aromatherapy for a condition she hadn't realized she had. She hadn't intentionally cut dating out of her life. It had come with the new job.

"I found out he plays Santa for the kids who are in the hospital over Christmas," Ty said.

Looking at him standing in her kitchen, his broad shoulders emphasized by the yoked style of his cream-colored Western shirt, she felt as if Santa had brought her an early present. "That's awesome!"

"I thought so. Made me feel good about buying the futon from him." He removed his hat. "Can I just put this on the counter? It needs to dry off a little."

"Sure. Anywhere." She would love to mess with his hair and get rid of the hat-brim crease.

"You don't have a lot of stuff sitting around." He laid his hat on the counter brim side up, cowboy-style. Then he finger-combed his damp hair, leaving it tousled and sexy looking.

"Just the espresso machine."

"I'd expect that. I meant you don't have a lot of doo-dads and whatchamacallits. Very streamlined. I like it."

"Thanks." Her list of things she liked about him was growing longer by the minute. "My mother thinks my apartment's stark, but I call it uncluttered."

"Less to move when you're cleaning."

"Exactly! And it's not like I spend a lot of time here, so I don't want to waste money buying a bunch of things I'll never use. My mom brought wineglasses when she and my dad came to visit in October, only to discover I didn't have a wine opener. I just buy screw-top."

Ty laughed, picked up the wine and opened it with a twist of his wrist. "I'm beginning to think we're twins."

"Sort of, yeah." Except that twins didn't always think alike. For instance, Selena would have decorated this apartment within an inch of its life. But now wasn't the time to think about that. She opened a cupboard, pulled out two of the pricey goblets from her mom and set them on the table.

"I took a chance on the wine. I didn't know if you

were into it, and if so, what you liked." He held up the bottle. "This is a Sauvignon Blanc. Is that okay?"

"Sounds good to me."

"Well, taste it and make sure you like it." He poured some in a glass and held it out to her.

"Is this the part where I'm supposed to swirl it around and stick my nose in the glass?"

He grinned. "Whitney, I do believe we're going to get along."

She met his gaze. "So do I." She drained the glass and returned it to him. "Fill 'er up while I get us plates, napkins and silverware." She turned back to the cupboard.

"Yes, ma'am. I asked them to include chopsticks, though, if you want to skip the silverware."

"I've never learned to eat with those, so I'll require a fork." She put cloth napkins, one of her few touches of elegance, on the plates. Then she opened another drawer and added utensils, including serving spoons for each carton.

"Want to learn how?"

She considered the prospect as she walked back to the table with the plates. Might be fun, considering who'd be teaching her. "Okay, why not?"

He'd unpacked the cartons and set them in the middle of the table. "See, I knew you were a woman with adventure in her soul."

"You did? Why?"

Opening each carton, he shoved a serving spoon in. "We could be meeting for a drink tonight, which would be the typical first step since we've never gone out. But you discarded that conservative move in favor of inviting me over to help with your tree."

A shiver of anticipation ran down her spine. "Too bold?"

"Nope. I loved it." He picked up both goblets and handed one to her before touching the rim of his glass to hers. "Thanks for asking me."

As she looked into his gray eyes and saw heat simmering there, her breath caught. Only minutes into this date she was already imagining what it would be like to kiss him. If the warmth in his gaze was any indication, he had kissing on his mind, too.

Instead he took a sip of his wine, and she followed his lead. The Sauvignon Blanc had a velvety taste that she liked very much. If she kissed Ty now, his lips would be flavored with wine. When he set his glass on the table, she wondered if she was about to have that experience.

Instead, he pulled out the chair across from him, the one that wasn't holding his coat. "Have a seat and I'll show you how to use chopsticks."

Good call. One kiss would likely turn into two, or ten. In the privacy of her apartment they had nothing and no one to interrupt them. She actually was hungry and she really did want to decorate her tree tonight.

Yet as he tore the wrapping from his chopsticks with his blunt-tipped fingers, excitement curled in her belly. Until now she hadn't realized how much she'd fantasized about this man. Having him all to herself for several hours didn't seem quite real. Maybe she could postpone the tree project.

He glanced up. "Ready?"

Now there was a loaded question. "You bet." Grabbing the wrapped chopsticks, she ripped off the paper and clutched one in each fist on purpose to make him laugh.

He did, which drew her attention to his mouth. He'd been blessed with lips that should be lovely to kiss, although shape meant nothing if he had no technique. That would be a crying shame. Until he proved her wrong, she'd assume he had excellent technique.

"Let's start with a piece of broccoli."

Oh, yeah. The chopstick lesson. "Broccoli's a good place to start." Using the chopsticks like pincers, she snatched a dark green clump from one of the cartons and deposited it on her plate.

His smile widened. "I thought you didn't know how to do this?"

"I don't, but obviously it's easier to grab ahold of something firm than something limp." In the dead silence that followed her cheeks grew warm. "I mean... when you're talking about...chopsticks." But there was no fixing this.

Lips pressed together, he glanced up at the ceiling. Then he dropped his head to his chest and a small snort escaped. His shoulders shook. Finally he gave up the fight and laughed until the tears came.

She couldn't blame him. Besides, his laughter was catching. Once she started in, it was hard to stop, especially whenever they looked at each other.

At last he wiped his eyes and drew a ragged breath. "I'll never look at broccoli and chopsticks the same way again."

"Me, either." She stifled a giggle. "Talk about an icebreaker."

"Yeah." He chuckled. "I'd say the ice is permanently smashed, and there wasn't much there to begin with. So." He smiled at her. "Still want to learn to use chopsticks?"

"If you don't teach me now, I'll never learn. If anybody else tried, they wouldn't understand why I keep cracking up."

"All righty. Let me take a restorative sip of wine and we'll begin again."

"I like your selections, by the way. I'm a fan of beef and broccoli and orange chicken."

"Somehow I'm not surprised." He gazed at her for a long moment.

Another few seconds of that intensity and she was liable to abandon dinner and suggest dessert, the most delicious kind she could imagine. Still, she thought they should hold off. This getting acquainted time was sweet and she didn't want a physical relationship to overpower it. "But if I'm going to eat anything besides broccoli, I need more instruction."

"Right." He balanced his set of chopsticks between his fingers. "Hold them like this. Use your thumb and forefinger to control the action." He plucked a piece of chicken out of the carton.

She was reasonably well coordinated, so after a few practice tries, she was able to pick up both the beef and the chicken and put them on her plate.

"Excellent."

"Yes, I did it, but at this rate I'll starve to death. I think I'll use a fork for the meal and practice later. I have the general idea." She peered at him. "Unless you're some kind of stickler who'll be offended."

"I'm a stickler when it comes to contract law and not much else. By all means, use a fork."

"But you won't, will you?"

He shrugged. "I'm used to eating with chopsticks. It's fun for me."

"Then by all means, go for it." She served herself a generous portion of each dish, plus a spoonful of brown rice. "Who taught you how to use them?"

"My mom."

The abbreviated response told her not to ask any more questions. The short bio on the calendar had mentioned that he'd lost both parents at fourteen, so it had likely been an accident of some kind. She understood how one tragic moment could change someone's life.

She and Ty didn't know each other well enough to delve into those dark recesses. But his mother had taught him well. He could manipulate those chopsticks as if he'd been born with them in his hand.

He picked up a clump of rice and held it effortlessly in midair. "The new location seems to be doing great."

Change of topic. That was fine with her. She nodded as she finished a bite of the excellent orange chicken. "It is. Ginny had high hopes that the town would be a good market, and it's turned out that way."

"I'm sure you had something to do with that." He popped the rice into his mouth.

"I hope so. I've always loved coffee shops. They've been gathering places for centuries. I feel as if I'm carrying on an important tradition."

"You definitely are. I've used Rangeland Roasters for meeting both clients and friends. It's a no-pressure spot to hang out."

"I know!" She warmed to her favorite subject. "I brought in some universal games like checkers and chess. My customers love them! And while they play, they drink coffee, so that means more revenue. Good for them and good for the shop."

"Besides that, you make them feel at home. You remember names and drink orders."

"Oh, that's easy."

"For you, maybe. Some people have a really tough time recalling names and personal details. Their brains are busy with stuff like quantum physics."

"Or contract law?" She knew he was smart, but she didn't have a grasp on what kind of smart.

"Thinking about a case doesn't keep me from remembering everyday things, especially if they're written down somewhere or I have a clear picture in my head."

"Photographic memory?"

"That's what the tests say."

That fascinated her. "Tell me how it works."

"I can't speak to how it works with others, but for me, if I need to remember something, I take a mental picture of it. That can be a page of case law or the items on this table."

"Perfect recall."

"If I concentrate, pretty much."

"Amazing. What a talent."

He smiled and shook his head. "Maybe, but I can't take credit for it. I was born that way." He hesitated. "So was my mom."

She accepted that admission as the gift it was. He trusted her enough to tell her something personal. All things considered, this date was off to a great start. "That's a nice legacy."

"That's what my foster mom said a long time ago. She was right, but then, she usually is. I guess you've met her."

"Rosie? Oh, yeah. She pops in at least once a week. Usually she orders a Mocha Madness, but every once in a while she'll have a Crazy for Caramel instead. She keeps telling me I need to get a liquor license so I can serve Baileys in her coffee."

He laughed. "She does love that combo. By the way, she and Herb, plus a couple of my brothers and their girlfriends, are out dancing tonight. We're invited, but I didn't make any promises."

"Oh!" Maybe she wouldn't have him all to herself, after all. He'd come to Sheridan to visit his foster family and they were off having fun without him. "Of course we can. I'll decorate my tree another time."

"But you'd set aside tonight to do it. I'll take a wild guess that the Friday after Thanksgiving is when you normally put up your tree."

"It is, but—"

"Then that's what we'll do. I want to. I haven't decorated a tree since I lived at Thunder Mountain."

"You don't put up one in your apartment?"

"I have a predecorated tree I haul out of the closet and plug into a timer."

She gazed at him. "That sounds very…practical."

"And boring?"

"I didn't say that."

"But tell the truth and the whole truth. You were thinking it."

She smiled. "Yes, your honor, I was. Okay, we'll decorate the tree, but it won't take long, and we can probably still meet your family afterward."

He polished off his wine and picked up the bottle to refill their glasses. "Maybe. Let's see how the evening goes."

And just like that, her mind went right back to thoughts of kissing him. If they stayed here, she had a much better chance of that happening.

4

TY WOULD LOVE to dance with Whitney, but not tonight. They were still figuring out whether this relationship had possibilities and he wanted to give them time to do that before getting involved with his family.

He could see why Rosie would think Whitney was perfect for him, though. Her openness and sense of humor definitely appealed to him. Whether he was perfect for her was a whole other question. He had a few issues. Near as he could tell, she didn't have any, or certainly not major ones.

Although he liked to think he'd handled his problems, his relationships never seemed to last very long. He knew he was picky, but still, he was a little surprised that he'd never come even close to proposing. Despite Rosie's intuition, Whitney could end up being another of his dead-end affairs.

Physically, though, they were like a pile of kindling waiting for a match. He couldn't speak for her, but he was trying to hold off. Although technically they'd known each other for almost a year, he wasn't sure those short conversations at Rangeland Roasters counted for much. They'd been more like teasers.

Yeah, that was a good word for those interactions, and maybe that explained why they were both so eager to get on with it. He could see it in her eyes. A couple of times he'd held her gaze a little too long and had felt a really strong urge to kiss her. He had a feeling she'd be fine with that.

But no matter what did or didn't happen between them, he'd be driving back to Cheyenne on Sunday. At first he'd considered that a negative, but now he could see the positive side of it. The attraction between them had built-in boundaries.

Considering how strong the chemistry was, boundaries might be a good thing. Driving back to Cheyenne would be like taking a recess during an intense trial. Nothing like a cooling-off period to allow those involved to reason more clearly.

He helped her clean up the kitchen, which was another test to see if he could keep his hands to himself. It was a compact kitchen and they weren't small people. Each accidental—or maybe not so accidental—brush of their bodies jacked up his pulse.

By now he had a clear and detailed mental image of her and he knew they'd fit together like puzzle pieces. More than once he wondered how she saw this evening ending. She'd been the one to suggest spending it in her apartment.

But she was naturally friendly, so coming here might have been a spur-of-the-moment idea because her time was so limited and she'd planned to trim the tree. Just because they had the opportunity for more than a casual evening together didn't mean they should act on it. They probably shouldn't, in fact.

He couldn't totally banish the thought, though. She smelled terrific, a spicy scent mixed with the aroma of

the brewed coffee she'd spent her day serving. Whenever she moved past him in the kitchen he could almost
taste that Peppermint Pleasure latte. He had a hunch
she'd taste even better.

Somehow they made it out of the kitchen and into the
living room without ending up in a clinch. Apparently
she'd been bold enough to invite him into her apartment
but she wasn't bold enough to make the first move, at
least not yet. That was good, because if she so much as
dropped a hint, he'd fold. A guy could only be so noble.

But she didn't hint. Instead she walked straight over
to her tree and crouched next to the cardboard box sitting beside it. Rosie and Herb had no set schedule for
putting up theirs, but his parents had always designated
the Friday after Thanksgiving for buying and trimming
the tree.

He'd be on vacation from school and they'd take off
work so all three of them could head for the tree lot first
thing in the morning for a better selection. Then they
waited until after dinner to trim it so they could see if
the lights were spaced right. He hadn't thought about
any of that in years.

She pulled out a strand of lights and looked up at him.
"I don't know if you have a favorite method, but—"

"I don't and besides, this is your tree. You get to be
in charge."

"Then lights go first." She handed him the strand.
"There's a plug right by the tree. I only have two of these,
but that should be enough."

"Should be." He leaned down and plugged in the
lights. The multicolored glow brought an unexpected
tightening in his throat. Damn, now was not the time
to get all mushy.

He never had when he'd helped with the Thunder

Mountain tree. But that had been a noisy, rowdy process filled with teasing and arguments among the guys about light and ornament placement. This intimate evening with just the two of them was a lot closer to his childhood Christmases.

"Good. They work." She stood. "If you'll unplug them for a minute, I'll be right back. I forgot to start the Christmas music."

He almost asked her to forget the music, but that wouldn't be fair. If she was anything like his folks had been, then she loved decorating a tree while listening to carols. He'd loved it, too. He could do this.

She left the room. Moments later, an instrumental version of *Silent Night* started up, and he sighed in relief. That wasn't the version his parents had played.

Funny, but he hadn't thought helping her with this would be any kind of problem after all these years. He held the strand of lights and waited for her to come back, but she was taking a while. Maybe she was checking her teeth for bits of Chinese food.

When she finally reappeared, she gave him a bright smile. "That's better. You can't decorate a tree without carols, right?"

"Right." Unless he was mistaken, her smile was a little *too* bright, almost as if she'd had to force it. And her mascara was slightly smudged, too. "Are you okay?"

"Yeah." She blew out a breath. "It's stupid, really. I'm almost twenty-seven years old and I've lived on my own ever since I graduated from college. But even after I moved out and had my own tree, I always went over to my folks' house to help with theirs. Hearing *Silent Night* got to me a little bit."

"Do you want to skip the music?"

"No! It's part of the tradition and I love Christmas

carols. I'll be fine. It's just that I've always been there so I have to get used to being here, instead."

"If you're sure, because I don't have to have it on."

"Well, I do." She sounded determined. "I can't imagine decorating a tree without Christmas music." Taking a deep breath, she gazed at him. "Ready to plug those lights in again?"

"You bet." Too bad he couldn't pull her into his arms for a sympathetic hug, but ironically he didn't know her well enough for that kind of friendly, nonthreatening embrace. When he took her in his arms for the first time, he didn't want her to wonder about his motivation.

He arranged the lights across the bottom front of the tree and halfway around the back. Then he placed what was left of the strand in her outstretched hand so she could continue around to the front again. That brief touch of her warm fingers made him long for more contact.

A few kisses would be okay, but he'd stop before things went too far. They were both feeling vulnerable, which wasn't a good way to begin a sexual relationship. Judging from the mood developing between them, he was fairly sure they would end up having one, even if they did live five hours apart.

"This would have been tougher working alone." She handed the lights off to him. "Come to think of it, when I trimmed my apartment tree in Cheyenne, I always roped somebody into helping me." She laughed. "So I'm continuing my pattern. Consider yourself roped in."

"Glad to do it." And he was, even if he'd had a bad moment at first. "I'm ready for the next set of lights."

He admired the ripple of her golden hair as she leaned over to pull out the second strand. He imagined running his fingers through it and gazing into her eyes. He wanted to taste those full lips. He closed his eyes briefly as he imagined how amazing that would feel.

"Ty?"

"Sorry." Caught. He took the lights she held out to him. "Got distracted." He joined the first set to the second and thought of the terminology for the connecting ends—male and female plugs. He and his foster brothers used to joke about that when they were raunchy teenagers who thought about sex constantly.

"You must have been thinking of something nice."

"I was."

She didn't pursue it, which probably meant she knew the sort of thing he'd been thinking about.

They traded the bunched cord back and forth, winding the lights around the branches until Ty looped the end at the top. Then they both stepped back and squinted at the lit tree to check placement.

"It's almost perfect," she said. "But there's a blank space in the middle."

"I see it." He stepped forward and adjusted one strand lower. Then he backed up. "I think that does it."

"I think so, too."

He heard something in her voice, something soft and yielding that made his heart beat faster. He glanced over at her. She was staring right back at him, her eyes dark and her breathing shallow. If any woman had ever looked more ready to be kissed, he'd eat his hat.

And damned if he could resist her. His gaze locked with hers and his body tightened as he stepped closer. Slowly he combed his fingers through hair that felt as silky as he'd imagined. "We haven't finished with the tree."

"I know." Her voice was husky. "And there's the dancing afterward…"

"We were never going to do that." He pressed his fingertips into her scalp and tilted her head back. "But I think we were always going to do this." And he lowered his head.

She awaited him with lips parted. After the first gentle pressure against her velvet mouth, he sank deeper with a groan of pleasure. So sweet, so damned perfect. She tasted like wine, better than wine, better than anything he could name.

The slide of her arms around his waist sent heat shooting through his veins. As she nestled against him, he took full command of the kiss, swallowing her moan as he thrust his tongue into her mouth.

She welcomed him, slackening her jaw and inviting him to explore. He caught fire, shifting his angle and making love to her mouth until they were both breathing hard and molded together. As he'd known, they fit exactly.

He registered the swell of her breasts, the curve of her hips and the press of her thighs. His cock hardened. The red haze of lust threatened to wipe out his good intentions, but he caught himself before he slid his hands under her sweater. Gulping for air, he released her and stepped back.

Looking into eyes filled with the same need pounding through him nearly had him reaching for her again. He fisted his hands at his sides. "Let's…maybe we should… back off for a bit."

She swallowed. "Okay. Care to say why?"

"I had a really valid reason a second ago."

She laughed. "It's a good thing you're so damned cute. I'll give you a minute to collect your thoughts."

"Thanks." He rubbed the back of his neck and struggled for clarity.

"You did say there's no girlfriend."

"Right. No girlfriend." Then he remembered why they needed to put the brakes on. Boy, she'd really fried his circuits. But the tree trimming had stirred up neediness in both of them. She might not be overly affected by it, but he was.

Saying all that out loud, though, would mean bringing up a touchy subject, one he wasn't prepared to discuss at the moment. Maybe a distraction was in order. "What's your schedule tomorrow?"

"My schedule? Why?"

"Humor me. What shifts are you working?"

"Most of them. Pretty much all day and for a couple of hours in the evening, too."

"Any breaks?"

"Yeah, for an hour between one and two and again from six to seven. Usually I eat something at my desk."

"Let me take you to lunch at one and dinner at six."

She blinked in obvious bewilderment. "You're kidding."

"No. We'll go to that little diner. It's close."

"For both meals?"

"You don't like the food?"

"I like it fine, but I'm confused. What's going on?"

"I…want to spend more time with you before we're in a kissing situation again."

A slow smile curved her kiss-reddened mouth. "Speaking of that, I'll leave the coffee shop at nine tomorrow night. Is there a chance you might want to drop by here after I'm off work?"

"If you'll have me."

"Now there's a loaded statement. How should I answer that?"

He groaned. "Don't try. You'll get us both in trouble.

I'll be at the shop at one." He walked toward the kitchen and got his coat.

"You're leaving?"

He grabbed his hat from the counter before turning to face her. "If I stay, I guarantee things will get out of hand."

"Not necessarily."

He gazed at her without speaking.

"Okay, you're right. That kiss was a barn burner. Dampened my panties."

He sucked in a breath. "Don't tell me that."

"Why not? You might as well know how you affect me since I'm well aware how I affect you. I was there, remember? I could tell what was going on with you."

"I'm sure you could."

Her gaze swept down to his crotch. "Still going on, I believe. When we have these pre-sex meals you're determined to share, you'd better keep your hands and knees to yourself or no telling what might happen in the privacy of our booth."

"Nothing will happen because we'll sit at the counter."

"Spoilsport."

"I'm just trying to—"

"I know." She sighed. "And I get it, actually. I need to stop giving you grief. Tonight's been emotional for me, and you don't want to take advantage when I'm feeling needy. But you won't say so because you're a true gentleman."

"No, I'm not."

"You are, Ty. You came over for a night of fun and games and instead you ended up with a woman getting teary and homesick over Christmas carols. Another guy might have seen that as an opportunity, but not you.

You'd rather get together when I'm feeling strong and happy. Am I right?"

"Sort of." His conscience was giving him hell. "For the record, I had a reaction to those carols, too."

"You did?"

"My folks and I always put up our tree on the Friday after Thanksgiving and played Christmas music while we did it."

She drew in a breath. "Oh, Ty. I'm so sorry. I should have realized that the holidays might be a tough time for you."

"They're not. It's been fourteen years since they died, and the plane went down in July. It wasn't a tragic accident during Christmas."

"Fourteen years might sound like a long time to some people, but it doesn't to me. And holidays can be difficult no matter when the tragedy happened."

"Thanks for that, but I'm pretty much at peace with losing them." He'd discovered that saying he was at peace usually kept people from feeling sorry for him.

"I'm glad."

"Besides, I enjoy Christmas. I hadn't put any importance on the Friday night tree decorating tradition, and I'm surprised it bothered me." He put on his hat and shoved his arms into the sleeves of his coat.

"Still, I wish I'd known."

"What if you had? I wouldn't have wanted you to change your plans because I might get upset." He gestured to the tree. "But I apologize for not finishing the job."

"The lights are the hardest part. I'll take care of the rest. It'll be all decorated when you come over tomorrow night."

"That sounds great." He dropped a quick kiss on her cheek and headed for the door. "See you at one."

"You don't have to take me out for two meals. That seems silly."

He turned back and smiled at her. "Just go with it, okay? I want chaperones to make sure we sit and talk."

"Does that mean we won't be talking tomorrow night?" She stood in the glow of the colored lights, her skin flushed and her breathing shallow. He'd never seen a sexier, more beautiful woman in his life.

He gripped the door handle to remind himself that he was leaving, by God. "Probably not much." And he walked out before he changed his mind.

5

SOMETIME AFTER ELEVEN the next morning, Rosie Padgett came through the door of Rangeland Roasters. Whitney wasn't terribly surprised to see Ty's foster mother. In Rosie's shoes, she would have done the same.

Rosie pushed back the hood of her down jacket and fluffed her blond hair as she walked toward the counter. Then she unzipped the jacket to reveal a red sweatshirt with "Dear Santa, I can explain…" lettered on the front.

Whitney laughed. "Nice sweatshirt."

"Couldn't resist it. Herb says it's so me."

"He should know. Mocha Madness today?"

"You know it, girlfriend."

"Anything else?"

"No, thanks. Ate too much apple pie yesterday." She took money out of her purse and handed it to Whitney. "But I really need the caffeine. Christmas shopping after this."

"Good for you. I haven't even started." Whitney rang up the coffee and turned to Meryl, who'd just finished making a Peppermint Passion order. "Are you caught up, or do you need me to make it?"

"I'm caught up." Meryl smiled. "Hi, there, Rosie."

"Hey, Meryl. Whitney's keeping you busy, I see."

"That's how I like it." She started putting together Rosie's drink.

"Busy is definitely good." Whitney was glad nobody had come in after Rosie, though. It gave her a chance to mention last night's invitation. "Sorry I didn't make it out dancing with everyone, but thanks for asking me."

"I was sorry, too. Ty said you were bushed after working all day."

"Um, yeah, sure was." That was as good an excuse as any and she appreciated Ty making one for her.

"Maybe another time. He's an excellent dancer. It's like being on *Dancing with the Stars*." She glanced behind her as more customers came in. "You may get too busy, but if you could come over and sit for a minute, that would be great."

"I will if I can." She'd love a woman-to-woman chat and she figured Rosie felt the same now that they had Ty Slater in common.

Rosie thanked Meryl for the coffee and carried it to a vacant table next to the window. In no time, Rosie's friend Harriet came through the door. Once Harriet had her coffee she joined Rosie and they began an animated conversation.

So much for a private discussion about Ty. Whitney should have realized that was unlikely. Rosie might come in alone most of the time, but she never stayed that way for long. She seemed to know everyone in town, and inevitably at least one friend would show up. More often it would be two or three.

But a little while later, Harriet's husband stopped in and they both left. Whitney put Meryl in charge of the counter and walked over to sit across from Rosie. "How was your Thanksgiving?"

"Wonderful. I'll bet you worked most of the day, didn't you?"

"I did, but no worries. I'm not martyring myself to the cause. I'll close on Christmas. I just promoted Meryl to assistant manager, so now I have someone to cover for me when I'm gone."

"Good call. She's a hard worker."

"And ambitious and intelligent. I lucked out with her. Anyway, she's taking Christmas Eve Day and the twenty-sixth for me. I'll drive down to Cheyenne to see my folks then."

Rosie nodded in approval. "Excellent. I'm sure they miss you."

"They do, and I miss them, but opening this new location is a terrific opportunity for me."

"You're doing a fine job, too. Incidentally, I'm glad you and Ty rediscovered each other."

"He's a great guy."

"I agree."

Whitney smiled. "I'm sure you do."

"I guess you're aware of his background because it was printed on the calendar. I'm still not sure how I feel about that. It helps the cause, but I think it bothers him for strangers to know those details. He hates the idea of being pitied. All my boys do."

"Personally, I admire him for getting on with his life the way he has. I'm sure you and Herb were a part of that healing process."

"We were, of course, but he had a good foundation. His parents were nice people. We knew them slightly, and my boys went to school with Ty, so naturally Herb and I wanted to help."

"He's lucky you were there for him."

"He knows that. At first he was mad at the world,

but he's mellowed out, thank goodness. That doesn't mean I don't worry about him." She reached over and patted Whitney's arm. "I'm thrilled you're seeing each other. He told me you have plans to get together today and later this evening, so I assume you're enjoying each other's company."

"We are." Her face grew warm.

Rosie grinned. "Now that's cute as all get-out. He turned pink, too, when I mentioned it. Anyway, that's really what I came in to say, that I'm happy for both of you. I didn't get a chance to tell you last night."

"Well, thank you." She took a steadying breath. "But I'm not sure how much we'll be seeing each other over the long haul, considering we live so far apart. A five-hour drive, especially in the winter, isn't all that much fun."

"I know the situation's not ideal, but these things have a way of working out if they're supposed to." Rosie's gaze shifted to a spot over Whitney's shoulder. "Hey, Janine! Saw you come in a minute ago. Recovered from all your dancing last night?"

Whitney turned as one of Rosie's oldest friends walked over to the table, coffee in hand. Whitney gave up her chair despite Janine's protest.

Meryl was due for her break soon, and Whitney wanted her to take it so she'd be back before one. Ty had shown up right on time last night and probably would again today. Although she'd called his plan silly, she could hardly wait to see him.

Ever since he'd given her that heated gaze before walking out her door, she'd been riding an adrenaline high. She'd finished trimming the tree while sipping wine from the bottle. There'd been at least a third of it left and they'd washed the goblets.

Then she'd put up her only other Christmas decoration, a ball of fake mistletoe. She'd chosen to hang it in the archway leading into her kitchen, but it didn't really matter where she put it. Kissing Ty was a foregone conclusion whether she had mistletoe or not.

She'd taken a hot bath in the vain hope that it would relax her. But who could be expected to fall asleep in a bed that probably would be occupied by a gorgeous cowboy in less than twenty-four hours? Finally she'd managed to doze off only to wake up superearly.

At least she'd had plenty of time to put fresh sheets on the bed and clean towels in the bathroom. The sheets were plain white. For a moment she'd wished for something less boring, but then she'd remembered how he'd looked at her.

He wouldn't notice the color of the sheets. All he'd require would be her naked body stretched out on a relatively soft horizontal surface. And all she'd require would be permission to caress his naked body as they made sweet love all night long.

Being at work had presented another challenge. She had trouble not staring at the calendar. Yes, she could see his sculpted chest even with her eyes closed, but that didn't mean she didn't want to study it some more.

That wasn't a good idea, though. Every time she glanced at Ty's picture, a shiver of anticipation ran through her. Sooner or later Meryl was liable to notice. Precisely at one, Ty strode into Rangeland Roasters. Today he wore typical wrangler clothes—jeans faded and softened with time and scuffed boots that had seen plenty of action in the barn and the corral. He had on the same shearling jacket and brown Stetson, but underneath he had on a blue chambray work shirt. The longer he was in Sheridan, the less he resembled an attorney.

He met her gaze and she felt the connection from the roots of her hair to the tips of her toes. She gave a short nod to let him know she'd be right with him. Then she ducked into her small office to grab her parka and her phone.

"It's all yours, Meryl," she said to her dark-haired assistant as she pushed her arms into the sleeves of her coat. "Call me if you have any problems."

"I won't." Meryl's quiet confidence had earned her the promotion. She was unflappable.

Whitney required that trait in order to feel comfortable putting someone else in charge of the shop. "Well, let me know if you do. I can be here in no time."

"Go have fun. You deserve it."

Whitney lowered her voice. "I don't know how much fun a girl can have in an hour."

"With a guy who looks like him? Plenty."

As Whitney walked toward Ty, she had to agree. His welcoming smile was a party all by itself. She gazed up at him. "Hi, you."

"Hi, yourself." Warmth flashed in his gray eyes.

"Rosie came in this morning."

He nodded. "I'm not surprised. I knew she drove in for some secret Christmas shopping. She's tickled about us."

"I could tell."

"I explained to her that dating isn't going to be a simple thing with you here and me down in Cheyenne, but she seems to think we can work around it."

She gazed at him and realized the distance between Sheridan and Cheyenne was shrinking in her mind. "We might."

"We just might. Time will tell. And speaking of time, we'd better get moving. The clock's ticking." With a hand against the small of her back, he guided her out the front door of Rangeland Roasters. Then he laced his fingers through hers and started off at a brisk pace toward the diner.

"Is this what they call speed dating?"

He slowed immediately. "Sorry. Guess I wanted to maximize the time I spend sitting next to you."

"At the counter, right?"

"Yes, ma'am." He squeezed her hand. "Especially after you gave me a vivid picture of what might happen in a booth. Besides, we'll get seated quicker and served faster. Do you know what you want?"

That gave her the giggles, and her breath frosted in the cold air. No more snow had fallen since Wednesday night, but the temperature still hovered around thirty degrees.

"I can see where your mind is." Laughter rippled in his voice.

"Do you blame me? You've strongly suggested that tonight we'll—"

"Maybe we shouldn't talk about that."

"Nobody's paying attention."

"Nobody except yours truly, and talking about it makes me want to do it, which has predictable anatomical consequences."

"*Predictable anatomical consequences?* Is that a legal term?"

"If it's not, it should be." He pushed open the door and ushered her into the diner. "And that subject's officially off-limits."

"You're no fun."

"That's where you're wrong. I just pick the appropriate time and place. This isn't it." He paused inside the door. "Good. The counter has spots available."

The hostess arrived and seated them immediately as

he'd predicted. The stools had backs, which gave them a place for their coats. Ty barely had time to help Whitney off with hers before two water glasses appeared along with napkins and silverware.

He gestured toward the glasses. "See? Counters rock." He took off his jacket and hung it on the back of his stool.

"Unless you want to fool around."

"Stop it." He bumped his knee against hers.

She bumped back. "I can't help it if you kissed me last night and gave me ideas."

He blew out a breath and stared straight ahead. "I am deliberately changing the subject. Is your tree decorated?"

"Yes." This time she rubbed her knee against his instead of bumping it. "And I hung up some mistletoe."

"Of course you did." He tugged on the brim of his hat. Then he gave her a sideways glance, amusement glinting in his eyes. "Did you really consider that necessary?"

"The knee rub or the mistletoe?"

"Both."

"No."

"I should hope not. The knee rub is overkill and any guy who's met you wouldn't need mistletoe to inspire him."

"That is a really fancy compliment, Ty. I'm not sure I've ever had such a fancy compliment." Or had one delivered by such a gorgeous hunk of manhood.

"See what I'm discovering about you with this lunch date? You have a smart mouth."

She met his gaze and lowered her voice. "Oh, Ty, you have no idea how smart my mouth can be." And she ran her tongue over her upper lip.

"Dear God." He glanced away and his jaw tightened. "What have I done?"

"Not only is my mouth smart, but it's educated." She bumped his knee again. "Do you understand what I'm saying, cowboy?"

He turned to her. "Do you realize you're torturing the man who's paying for your lunch?"

"Let me remind you that this lunch plan was your idea and not mine. Last night I was perfectly willing to—"

"Enough." His large hand closed over her thigh and squeezed. "We're going to talk about neutral topics while we eat the burgers and fries which are coming our way."

His warm hand on her thigh was doing crazy things to her pulse rate, but she pretended total nonchalance. "Would you care to make a list of acceptable subjects?"

"You know what I'm saying." He glanced up as plates were put in front of them. "Be nice."

"I am nice. Very nice. As you'll quite likely find out later."

"Whitney, do you have a one-track mind?" He gazed into her eyes.

She could get lost in those gray depths. "Today I do. Don't you?"

"God help me, yes. But I thought that getting together like this would diffuse things a little."

"Wrong."

"So I see. Eat your lunch." He turned away, picked up his burger in both hands, and took a generous bite.

It shouldn't have been a sexy move, but with Ty every move was sexy, even chewing. His jaw was clean-shaven, unlike the scruff he'd worn for the calendar. "Who decided you should have a beard for the calendar picture?"

"The photographer." He glanced pointedly at her untouched meal and lifted his eyebrows.

"Okay, okay." She focused on her plate and began eating her burger.

He went back to his food, too, but after swallowing another bite, he spoke. "Just FYI, don't expect a tan. That was taken in the summer. I'd spent some weekends at the ranch helping Rosie and Herb spruce up the place."

"Nobody has a natural tan in Wyoming in the winter. I was just curious about the beard because I've only seen you clean-shaven."

"Well, there's no way I'll have that kind of scruff by tonight, either." He sounded mildly irritated.

Puzzled by his tone, she put down her burger and looked at him. "I'm not expecting you to show up with a beard."

"That's good." Instead of meeting her gaze, he pretended great interest in his pile of French fries before finally choosing one.

"Is something bothering you?"

"I just hope to hell this isn't about the calendar." He looked at her. "Because that's not who I am."

"What do you mean by *this*?"

"What's going on between you and me."

"Oh." Now she felt a little guilty for all the times she'd stared at the calendar and fantasized about him.

"You see, Dominique—she's the photographer—wanted a certain look, especially because I'd be on display first and the picture needed to be a grabber. She suggested the scruff and setting up our session at dawn. Then she kept shooting until she got the expression she wanted, as if I'd just rolled out of bed and left behind a very satisfied woman."

Whitney hadn't consciously thought about it, but now that he'd described the intent behind the shot, she had to agree the subtle implication was there. "She nailed it."

"Apparently. I've been propositioned by women who

expect me to be... I don't know. Out of the ordinary.
I'm not."

Her heart ached for him. She'd never considered that
such a sexy image would create an unrealistic expecta-
tion, or that it would bother him that he might not live
up to it. "I was attracted to you long before I saw that
calendar."

"Yeah?"

"Yeah." She laid a hand on his arm. His very warm,
solid arm. Squiggles of excitement danced in her stomach. "Knowing you're a lawyer who's also a cowboy on
the side is kind of fun, but I would have asked you to
help with my tree even if I'd never seen that calendar."

He studied her for a moment, and then he let out a
slow breath. "I'm sorry." He covered her hand with his.
"I probably overreacted. It's been a long four months."

"I can tell. But it's almost over."

"Thank God."

"And I know for a fact you created interest in the
program."

"That's what I keep telling myself, and that does help,
but it's somebody else's turn." He glanced at a clock
hanging on the wall and squeezed her hand. "Better eat
up. Time's flying."

"Right." She dived into her meal and vowed not to
mention the calendar ever again.

But she thought Ty's view of himself as ordinary was
way off the mark. He'd survived losing both parents and
from all indications was doing well in a demanding profession. She didn't see anything ordinary about him.

Besides, that cocky grin the photographer had coaxed
out of him had come from somewhere. It wouldn't hurt
for him to let that devilish streak out once in a while.
She wouldn't mind being around when he did.

6

ON THE DRIVE back to the ranch, Ty saw Rosie's truck up ahead. She must have finished with her Christmas shopping. If he passed her, he could beat her to the rural mailbox so she wouldn't have to stop for the mail. He couldn't save her the trouble every day, but he could do her a favor this afternoon.

She didn't drive fast, so catching up and passing wasn't tough. He beeped the horn on his way around and she honked back. Turning in at the ranch road, he glanced at the new sign Damon and Phil had made last summer.

THUNDER MOUNTAIN RANCH was carved into a slab of wood suspended between two sturdy posts about five feet high. Hanging beneath it was a smaller painted sign announcing Home of Thunder Mountain Academy, and under that hung an evergreen wreath decorated with pinecones and a big red waterproof bow. Both signs and the wreath looked as if someone had decided to add some whipped cream to the top edges.

Parking carefully along the side of the snow-packed dirt road, Ty climbed out and took a picture with his phone. It was Thunder Mountain Academy's first Christmas, and although no students would arrive until January, he thought this holiday deserved to be commemorated.

Rosie pulled up beside him and rolled down the window. "Were you planning to get the mail or just stand around taking pictures?"

He glanced over his shoulder. "Take pictures *and* get the mail."

"Then I'll wait here. We've been expecting word from the state as to whether students can use a semester at the academy for high school credit."

Shoving his phone in his coat pocket, he walked the short distance to the main road and the mailbox. Sure enough, one of the envelopes had the state seal on it.

His boots crunched on the packed snow as he walked back to Rosie's truck. "This might be it." He handed her the envelope.

"Looks like it!" She ripped it open and unfolded the sheets of paper. "Woo-hoo! We're approved!"

"Hey, that's great!" He was happy for her and everyone connected with the project, but he suspected what was coming next and it could seriously mess with his plans.

"We need to celebrate!" Then she glanced at him. "Hey, I didn't mean you. You have a date with Whitney tonight."

"No problem. I'll bring her out here."

"Would you do that?"

"Sure. I'll bet she'd want to celebrate with you. After all, she talked her boss into backing the project, so she's invested in the success of it, too." He had no idea if Whitney would embrace this change of plans. But she was an easygoing person so she probably would, even if she'd been eager to be alone with him. Hell, he'd been eager for that, too.

But this piece of paper was superimportant to his foster family. He couldn't justify spending the entire evening at Whitney's while everyone at Thunder Mountain was toasting their latest triumph. He'd ask her during dinner and see what her reaction was.

After handing over the rest of the mail, he got back into his truck and followed Rosie to the ranch. She parked around back in the garage, but he left his truck out front in the circular drive. He'd considered staying in town this afternoon and doing some Christmas shopping of his own, but in the end he'd decided to come back for a couple hours to be with Rosie and Herb.

If Rosie hadn't been so enthusiastic about his connection with Whitney, he would have worried about stealing time from his foster parents to see her. But Rosie had insisted on shopping alone today, anyway. She'd also made it plain this morning that she'd rather have him find the love of his life than hang out with her.

He'd made a halfhearted attempt to talk her out of that *love of his life* business, but once she got that concept into her head, no one could dislodge it. Others more experienced than he was had tried and failed.

Herb was as excited about the news as Rosie had been. While Rosie figured out the menu, which would largely be Thanksgiving leftovers, Herb called everyone who might be able to show up for the festivities. Ty offered to run the vacuum and straighten up the house in preparation for another party. Every foster brother was a good hand with a vacuum cleaner and a dust rag. Rosie had demanded it.

By the time he left to meet Whitney at Rangeland Roasters, the house and the food were ready. Herb was setting up the bar while Rosie changed into a sparkly sweater and red jeans for the occasion. If Whitney chose not to come out here after the coffee shop closed at nine, then he'd drive back to the ranch after having dinner with her.

That would change the dynamic between them, and the potential for getting together tonight might disappear. He'd take that chance. Whitney made him smile and she turned him on more than any woman he'd dated in a long time. But for one thing, she lived nearly five hours away. For another, they'd barely scratched the surface when it came to getting acquainted. The geographical distance was going to make the getting acquainted part tough.

But when he walked into Rangeland Roasters at exactly six o'clock and was greeted by her warm smile, his heart turned over. Whenever he was with her, something inside him clicked into place. Although he wanted her desperately, that wasn't the only reason he couldn't wait to see her. He just plain liked her. Even if they couldn't be lovers, he'd want to be her friend. That was a new situation for him.

On the way to the diner he wrapped an arm around her shoulders because it was freezing on the street. Huddled together, they didn't try to make conversation until they were seated at the counter again. They both ordered coffee this time.

"I want something besides a burger," she said. "Two in one day is one too many."

"Mac and cheese." Ty closed his menu.

"Perfect." She slapped hers closed. "Make that two."

He smiled at her. "I've known ladies who would shudder at the thought of mac and cheese."

"Really? Why?"

"Calories."

"Pfft." She waved a hand dismissively. "I'm on my feet for countless hours a day. If I ever quit working at Rangeland Roasters, I might have to watch my diet, but I'm running from the minute I hit the door until I lock up. I don't worry about calories."

"From where I sit, you don't have to."

"Thanks, Ty. That's the gentlemanly thing to say and I appreciate it. My clothes still fit, so that's all that concerns me. I don't make enough to buy a whole new wardrobe."

"Then it's mac and cheese for both of us." He ordered when the waitress came by.

"Before I forget, let me give you these." She pulled two keys on a small ring out of her pocket and handed them to him. "The big one's for the outside door and the smaller one is to my apartment. I don't know what you planned to do between dinner and coming over, but it's silly for you to sit in some bar passing the time. Just go on over and let yourself in."

"I was going to sit in some bar, but actually, the original plan isn't going to work."

"Oh?" She straightened. "Why not?"

He filled her in on the news. "Rosie's having a celebration, and I…need to be there. If you're willing to come with me after you close up tonight, that would be great, but I can understand if you—"

"Of course I will."

"Really? I'm afraid it jacks up our evening."

She smiled. "You'll have to bring me back to my apartment sometime, right?"

"Eventually." He held her gaze. "But you were up early and we're talking about a really long day. You might want me to drop you off and head for home."

"I changed the sheets on my queen-size bed. I'd hate to go to all that trouble for nothing."

He swallowed. "You make a good point."

"So we won't have an entire evening together. That could be a blessing if we don't…if we're not…compatible."

He couldn't help smiling at that. "I seriously doubt that will be the case."

"I seriously doubt it, too. Bottom line, do you really want to drive back to Cheyenne tomorrow without…"

"*No.*" His response came out with a little more force than necessary. He lowered his voice. "No, I don't."

"Me, either. But you need to celebrate with your foster family and I'd love to be there. I'll just need a few minutes to change clothes and then we can go."

Now that the keys to her apartment rested in his suddenly sweaty palm, he wondered how that would work, with her changing clothes while he was there. "The party might run late."

"Doesn't matter." She looked into his eyes. "I have a feeling that once we get back to my apartment, we won't be tired anymore."

As he imagined that explosive moment, he wasn't capable of coherent speech, so he made a little noise of agreement deep in his throat.

"But you probably need to make sure that nobody expects you to come home until morning."

"They won't."

"You're sure?"

He nodded. "Rosie wasn't born yesterday."

"All righty, then. I have to be at work at eight."

"That early? Then maybe we shouldn't—"

"We definitely should. I'm only telling you because

sometime around six-thirty, I'll need to shower and get dressed. But until then, I'm all yours."

He clutched the keys so tightly they bit into his palm. "But…" He paused to clear his throat. "But you'll be working most of the day. You need sleep."

"I live in the land of constantly available caffeine. You're the one who has to drive down to Cheyenne tomorrow. Can you go back to the ranch and take a nap first?"

"Absolutely." Or he'd mainline coffee all during the trip. He was worried about her lack of sleep, but not his. He'd made it through law school. He'd be fine—more than fine.

Her eyes grew as dark as melted chocolate. "Then I think we have a plan, cowboy." She motioned to the dishes that had appeared in front of them. "Now eat your mac and cheese. You have to keep up your strength."

He pocketed her keys and tucked into his meal, although he could barely taste it as anticipation sizzled in his veins. He'd presented the situation, and she'd reacted exactly as he'd hoped. They'd attend the celebration, and then…he forced himself to think of something else. Otherwise he'd have to deal with those predictable anatomical consequences again.

"Watch TV if you want while you wait for me," she said between bites.

"Okay. Thanks."

"I wish I could offer you a beer or some wine, but I don't have any. I drank the rest of the wine after you left."

"I'm glad you did. I was going to pick some up for us to have tonight, but now it doesn't make much sense."

"No, it doesn't. We won't have time to be drinking wine."

She made the statement so earnestly that it struck him

as funny. He turned to her with a grin. "Do you have a schedule mapped out?"

"You know what I mean. We have limited time and—"

"Lots to accomplish?"

Cheeks pink, she rolled her eyes. "Never mind."

"If you have a list, I should probably have a look at it."

"I should make one, just to shut you up."

"By all means. Then I won't waste precious minutes on things you'd rather skip."

She locked her gaze with his. "I don't want to skip *anything.*"

Just like that, she turned the tables on him. His body tightened and his breath came faster. "Sounds like a long list."

"You'd better believe it." With a gleam of victory in her eyes, she turned away and began eating again. Only a slight quiver of the fork in her hand indicated that she might have stirred herself up, too.

They left the diner soon after that and he walked her to the coffee shop. He considered kissing her goodbye outside the door but thought better of it. She wouldn't want to go into work looking kissed.

So he squeezed her hand and let her go. "See you soon."

"Looking forward to it."

"Me, too."

"Bye." She smiled and turned away.

He watched her step inside and immediately she started interacting with customers sitting at the tables she passed. She was a natural at a service-oriented job, but she'd excel at anything that involved meeting the public. His mom and dad would have loved her.

Where had that thought come from? He couldn't remember ever thinking that about any woman he'd dated. It was a pointless fantasy to have, anyway.

As he left the coffee shop, he turned his collar up against the bite of the wind and tugged his hat down over his eyes. The wind was making them water. That was his story and he was sticking to it.

But damn it, he really did want his folks to meet Whitney. Whitney would have loved them, too. Pointless fantasy or not, he couldn't seem to get the idea out of his head.

He'd just started to notice girls around the time they died, but he hadn't talked about it to either of them. His mom must have noticed, though, because she'd commented that soon he'd be glad for the ballroom dancing lessons she'd foisted on him. He'd secretly had fun taking them although he'd complained long and loud every week. He was good at it, better than any other guy in the class.

And he had been grateful for the lessons once he'd started going to dances in high school. A fast two-step lifted his heart and made him forget everything but the music. He wished he could have told his mom that she'd given him a tool that had helped a whole lot.

Once he was in his truck, he cranked up the heater and started toward Whitney's apartment. Then, on impulse, he turned down the street that would take him into his old neighborhood. He never drove by the house, but tonight he felt the urge to test himself and see what happened.

Slowing the truck, he leaned down to gaze through the window at the two-story house where he'd spent the first fourteen years of his life. Lights were on and whoever lived there now had put up Christmas decorations.

The roof was lined with multicolored bulbs and a blow-up Santa and sleigh sat in the small front yard.

The front walk was shoveled and the house looked taken care of. That was good. He wouldn't have wanted the place to get run-down. Tension that had gathered in his chest eased. He'd seen the house and hadn't been hit with a tidal wave of grief.

He continued on to Whitney's apartment complex with a sense of accomplishment, as if he'd jumped a hurdle he'd been avoiding for years. He told everyone he was at peace with losing his parents because then they tended to leave the subject alone. He wasn't about to let anyone dig into his past and open up old wounds.

Whitney seemed sensitive to that. Helping decorate her tree had skimmed the surface of his past like a light breeze over tall grass. He'd felt the memories stir, which was probably why he'd had the wayward thought about her meeting his parents and why he'd felt like driving by his old house.

Apparently he could handle that kind of gentle visit to his previous life without falling apart. He was relieved to find that out because being around Whitney seemed to cause random memories to surface. But just because he'd survived helping with her tree and seeing his childhood home didn't mean he wanted to unpack the photo albums stored in the back of his closet.

Theoretically he should be able to recall every page in those albums, but he couldn't remember a single picture or even what his parents had looked like. A guy with a photographic memory should be able to visualize his own parents, but he couldn't. He'd never told anyone that, not even Rosie. Sure as the world she'd have pushed him to see a therapist. No thanks.

Once he'd arrived in her apartment, he heard nothing

from her neighbors. Good soundproofing. Wouldn't have to worry about waking the neighbors later on tonight.

The living room felt like Christmas with the glow from the tree lights and the scent of pine in the air. Crouching down, he saw a timer in the wall plug. He used a timer for his artificial tree so he was greeted by lights every night when he came home, but maybe he should think about getting a real tree this year. He'd forgotten how great they smelled.

As he took off his coat, he admired the job she'd done with the decorations. Wired red ribbon had been woven through the branches and the little teddy bear anchored to the top made him smile. Glass snowflakes and icicles sparkled in the light and the ornaments all were different.

Leaving his coat and hat on the futon, he checked them out and soon realized each bore a different date. He counted twenty-seven It didn't take a genius to figure out that she had one for each year of her life. Nice. In a way he was glad he hadn't helped put them on. Accidentally dropping one would have been bad.

So, here he was in her apartment. He could sit down and watch TV, which sounded boring, or he could prowl around a little, which sounded way more fun. He knew what the kitchen was like, but there was an important room he'd never seen. She'd given him her keys so she had to know he'd take a look.

Heading down a short hallway, he came to her darkened bedroom. No timed lights in here. He patted the wall beside the door and found a switch. When he flipped it, two bedside table lights came on and illuminated a bed so inviting that he hated not having her here right this minute.

The headboard was some kind of reddish wood, maybe cherry, and the fluffy comforter was dark green.

It had been folded back, along with the white top sheet to reveal the snowy bottom sheet. Pillows in white cases had been stacked against the headboard—six of them, to be exact.

It wasn't the fanciest bed he'd ever seen, but it was the most tempting. Then again, he probably thought so because he was picturing Whitney lying naked in it. Crossing the room, he stroked his hand across a section of the bottom sheet. Nice and soft. Perfect to make love on.

He'd bought condoms yesterday, just in case. The box was in his truck, but he'd put two in each of his front jeans pockets before coming up here tonight. He'd love to leave them in here instead of carting them around all night, but where?

Putting them in one of the bedside table drawers seemed too much like snooping, but leaving them lying on top was too blatant. Finally he decided to open a drawer and toss them in. He wouldn't look at anything in there.

But when he opened the drawer, an entire box of condoms was already inside. He picked it up and discovered it had never been opened. She'd obviously been shopping recently, too.

Chuckling, he added his loose packets to the drawer and closed it. At least they wouldn't run out. Still smiling, he walked back into the living room. Just as he picked up the remote for her TV, the intercom buzzed.

Damn, he hoped she didn't have an unexpected visitor. Then he had to laugh at himself. It was probably Whitney, who'd given him her key and now needed to be buzzed in. Maybe someone was covering her last hour for her.

In that case, they had an hour in which no one expected them to be anywhere. Talk about an answer to his prayers. They might not have to wait until after the party, after all.

He opened the intercom connection. "Whitney?"

The silence that followed was not promising. "No, this is her mother. Who are you?"

7

THANK GOD MERYL had been willing to cover for her. As Whitney drove home, she tried to figure out her best approach to this fustercluck. A surprise visit from her mom and dad had never occurred to her, but maybe it should have.

When her mother had called a few minutes ago, she'd said they'd come up to surprise her with Thanksgiving leftovers. Whitney had never been away for Thanksgiving before, so that was a semireasonable explanation. Her mom had said they'd tried her apartment first and had been prepared to drive to Rangeland Roasters if they hadn't found her at home.

Knowing her parents and their love of tradition, they might have decided on a whim to make the ten-hour round trip to bring her turkey, cranberry sauce and pumpkin pie. Her dad might believe that rationale, but Whitney didn't buy it. After that Thanksgiving Day conversation, Ellen Jones had wanted to find out if anything was going on between her daughter and *the guy from the calendar*, which is how she'd referred to Ty on the phone just now.

Mentioning him had been a huge mistake. Because

she'd gone to college in Cheyenne, her parents had met everyone she'd ever dated. But *the guy from the calendar* was an unknown, and to be fair, he looked like a rascal in that shot.

So delivering Thanksgiving leftovers was a cover story and the actual reason was currently sitting in her living room sweating out an unexpected face-to-face with her parents. Poor Ty. She hadn't meant to put him in this position. She'd had several other positions in mind, though, and now that was a lost cause.

Because Ty had her front-door key, she used the intercom to get buzzed in.

Her dad answered. "Hey, sweetie! We're making turkey sandwiches and drinking a really good pinot noir. Come on up and join the party!"

"Be right there!" Oh, boy. They would assume she'd want turkey sandwiches on the Saturday after Thanksgiving because she always had before. She wondered if Ty was forcing down a sandwich to be sociable even though he'd had a large helping of mac and cheese not very long ago.

Her mother came out of the hallway and hurried to meet her. "Honey, I had no idea you would be seeing him again tonight. But once we were here, what could we do? He seems nice."

"He is nice, Mom." She gave her mother a hug. "And surprising me with Thanksgiving leftovers is a sweet and thoughtful idea."

"I actually wanted to find out what was going on with this new guy."

Whitney laughed. "I knew that."

"So you're not surprised we showed up?"

"I was at first, but when I thought about it on the drive home, I figured it out."

"Forgive me?"

"Of course." She smiled at her petite mother, whose head was a smidgen higher than Whitney's shoulder. Her parents were physical opposites, and Whitney had inherited her height from her dark-haired dad. Her coloring came from her mother, who was just beginning to go gray.

"I debated with myself for a long time after we talked on Thanksgiving, but in the end, I had to come up here. I trust your judgment, but I heard that homesick note in your voice, and here you were inviting this rakish-looking centerfold person into your apartment. You've never lived this far away before, and I just…needed to see for myself that you were okay."

"I understand, Mom." She wrapped an arm around her mom's shoulders as they walked back to the apartment. "Did Ty mention the celebration at his foster parents' ranch?"

"He did, just a little bit ago. Had we known about that we wouldn't have given him so much wine."

"So much wine? Is he drunk?"

"I don't think so. He's a big guy, and I fed him a turkey sandwich so that should help, but I gather you were supposed to go to this party at the ranch, too. You should go so you can drive him just in case he's not up to it. We'll hang out here until you get back."

Whitney had to press her lips together to keep from laughing. This was not the evening she'd been looking forward to. "I'll see what he thinks." She mentally added the mac and cheese to the turkey sandwich. Considering he'd only had about thirty minutes to eat a sandwich and drink wine, he couldn't have consumed that much. "But you've come all this way and I know you'll have to start back tomorrow, so I hate to run off and leave you."

"Ty has to head back to Cheyenne tomorrow, too, doesn't he?"

"Yes. Monday's a work day for him."

"Then you two should go to the party tonight regardless of which one of you drives. That's what you planned and that's what you need to do. I'm feeling like a buttinski right now."

"Don't worry about it. I don't have to go unless Ty's not okay to drive."

"But you should." Her mom pulled her back from the door and lowered her voice. "He's nothing like I thought he would be. Your dad and I have been talking with him and he's a lot more modest and gentlemanly than I expected. He's also smart and funny. I can see why you like him."

Whitney weighed her options. If she stayed here with her parents, she wouldn't get to spend any more time with Ty before he left. He'd drive to the ranch and that would be the end of that. She hated to leave things that way after all the plans they'd made.

"Okay, I'll go to the party," she said. "Please don't wait up for me, though. It could be late. And take my bed."

"I knew you'd want to give us your room, so we already have our stuff in there. Your bed looked as if you'd just changed the sheets."

Yikes. Her mother was way too observant. "You taught me well! I change the sheets every Saturday come hell or high water." Or a handsome cowboy.

"Well, I'll wash them again in the morning so you have fresh sheets for the rest of the week."

"You don't have to."

"No, I want to. It's the least I can do after all this. What time do you work tomorrow?"

"I start at eight, but I only scheduled myself for three hours and I don't go back until four. We can have a nice lunch before you drive home."

"Sounds perfect. Now let's go see what those men are up to. Last I heard, they were debating who would end up in the Super Bowl."

Whitney relaxed a little. If Ty could talk football with her dad, then they'd get along fine. Maybe it hadn't been a tortuous half hour for him, after all.

But when he met her gaze, he looked like a drowning man who'd just been thrown a lifeline. Good thing she'd decided to go to the party with him. They needed some time alone to sort this out.

He stood and set down his empty glass next to a half-eaten sandwich. On her dad's end table stood one empty wine bottle and one that was half full. Maybe she'd better drive, after all.

Her mother had obviously claimed the rocker. One of Whitney's little folding tables held her mom's glass and a partly eaten sandwich. Four people made her little apartment bulge at the seams.

Her dad came over and gave her a hug. "We just barged in here like we have good sense. Apparently you have plans, so you should go ahead with them."

"That's what I told her," her mother said.

"No worries. She certainly doesn't have to go." Ty picked up his coat and hat. "I'll just head out and let you enjoy time with your daughter."

Whitney unzipped her coat. "Actually, I'd like to go with you if that's still okay."

"You would?"

"I feel a connection to that project and I'd love to be part of the celebration. My folks will understand."

"We certainly will." Her mother smiled at Ty. "It's a

wonderful idea, this Thunder Mountain Academy. We made a small contribution, ourselves."

Ty looked confused. "Would you two like to come along, then? The more, the merrier."

"Oh, no." Whitney's father shook his head. "We've been on the road for five hours. Another glass of pinot noir and I'll be ready to turn in."

"Me, too." Her mom picked up her goblet. "You and Whitney go have fun."

Whitney glanced at Ty. "I'll just be a minute. I'd rather not go in my work clothes." She hurried into her bedroom and made the fastest wardrobe change in history.

Her parents' overnight bag stood in a corner and their jackets lay on the bed. Her mom's purse was on the dresser. Just in time, Whitney remembered the box of condoms she'd stashed in the bedside table drawer.

Yes, they knew she was a sexually active adult, but that didn't mean she wanted them to open the drawer and find that box, especially now that they were aware she'd given Ty her keys. She grabbed the box and noticed four loose packets of a different brand lying on top.

She had a tough time not bursting into hysterical laughter as she scooped those up, as well. Stuffing Ty's contribution in one of her slippers, she shoved the box behind a pair of rain boots. Next time she planned a hot night of sex, she'd make damned sure that her parents weren't about to visit.

Dressed in a black cowl-necked sweater and a new pair of jeans with rhinestones on the pockets, she ducked into her bathroom across the hall, quickly brushed her teeth and put on fresh lipstick.

She dropped her lipstick in her purse, picked up her coat and walked into the living room. All conversation stopped. Maybe they hadn't been talking about her, but she had a feeling they had. She glanced at Ty. "Ready?"

"Sure thing." He popped up immediately and came over to help her with her coat. "Just let me take my dishes into the kitchen."

"Leave them, leave them." Her mother made a shooing motion with her hand. "We'll take care of it. Have a great time."

"Thanks." Ty grabbed his jacket from where it lay on the futon and shrugged into it, his movements uncharacteristically clumsy. "It was really nice meeting you both."

"Nice to meet you, too." Her dad stood and they shook hands. "Five bucks says my team takes home the Super Bowl trophy."

"You're on." Ty reached for his hat.

"We'll be in bed by the time you get back." Whitney's mom stood and walked over to Ty. "So let me give you a goodbye hug, now."

"Sure thing." He looked startled but hugged her gently as if afraid she might break. He was no taller than her dad, but he was a lot more muscular. Her mom looked tiny in his arms.

"Now be on your way." She smiled at Whitney. "And I do think you'd better drive, honey." She rolled her eyes toward the two wine bottles on the end table.

"We'll see." But after watching Ty put on his coat and noticing the odd tilt of his hat, she had to agree. "I'll catch up with you two in the morning. Sleep well." She walked out the door Ty held open for her. Once it was closed behind them, she turned to him. "Would you like me to drive?"

"Yes, ma'am, I surely would."

"How much wine did you drink, anyway?"

He looked sheepish. "I'm not positive. Art kept refilling my glass when it started getting low and I was glad for that, to be honest. All of us were nervous and the wine helped. I didn't get around to mentioning the party at the ranch until right before you got home, so they probably thought the four of us would be hanging out together tonight."

"What if I hadn't decided to come with you?"

"I would have stopped somewhere for coffee and waited until I felt more like making the drive. Not Rangeland Roasters, obviously. Maybe the diner."

"Oh, Ty." She tucked her arm through his as they started down the hall. "I'm so sorry. I never dreamed they'd show up tonight. I'll bet you were in shock."

"Pretty much. But so were they. Things were tense at first, but then Art opened the wine and Ellen made sandwiches. They were so dead set on giving me food and booze that I couldn't decide how to bring up the subject of the party at first. Anyway, I was mighty glad to see you come through that door."

"I could tell." As they navigated the stairs, she realized that he wasn't his usual steady self.

"It was good wine," he said as they walked outside. "I'm going to look for that label. Went down real easy."

"I see that."

"Your mom seems to be the wine buyer in the family."

"She is. My dad's happy with whatever she picks out. Oh, by the way, I hid the condoms in my closet."

He stopped abruptly on the sidewalk. "Oh, God. I forgot about those. Did you get mine, too?"

"Yes." She grinned at him. "What did you think when you opened that drawer?"

He laughed. "That we had the same idea and we sure as hell wouldn't run out. Thanks for hiding them."

"No doubt my folks have guessed what we had in

mind for tonight, but I didn't want to hit them in the face with the evidence." She gave his arm a squeeze. "Well, there's my car, the burgundy Subaru."

"I see it." He walked her to the driver's side like the gentleman he was.

Fishing out her keys from her purse, she pressed the remote. She expected him to open the door for her, but instead he shoved back his hat with his thumb and reached for her.

"Before we climb in there, do you have some lipstick in your purse?"

"Why? Want to refresh yours?"

"Very funny. I desperately want to kiss you." His face was in shadow, but there was no mistaking the tight line of his jaw.

Her blood heated, making her forget the icy chill surrounding them. "That would be okay with me."

"I mean really kiss you, with full body contact." He stepped back and unbuttoned his jacket.

"Don't tell me you're taking that off."

"Nope." Leaving his jacket open, he unzipped her coat with surprising dexterity considering all the wine he'd had. Sliding his arms inside, he pulled her against his taut body. "I just don't want all that material between us."

"Yeah, this is much nicer." Heart pounding, she followed his lead and slipped her arms inside his sheepskin jacket. Then she gazed up at him. "I'm sorry this turned into such a mess."

He cinched her in closer. "My fault. You were ready to go for it last night." His breath fogged the air. "Wish we had."

She was ready to go for it now, and so was he, judging from the hard ridge pressed against her belly. But she wouldn't let him take the blame for their frustrating situation. "Waiting was the right thing to do, even if to-night didn't turn out the way we'd hoped."

"Keep telling yourself that." He lowered his head. "See if you believe it a few minutes from now." His hungry mouth found hers.

It took mere seconds before she deeply regretted last night's missed opportunity. Apparently the wine had stripped away his inhibitions, because his kiss was blatantly suggestive, far more sexual than the one he'd given her the night before. He tasted of wine and hot desire.

The steady stroke of his tongue drove her wild, sending a rush of warm moisture between her thighs. Despite the cold and the very public setting, she wanted to rip his clothes off so she could touch him everywhere. She moaned and snuggled closer.

He lifted his lips a fraction from hers. "I know," he murmured. "I know." Reaching under her sweater, he cupped her breast through the lace of her bra.

Whimpering, she arched her back and silently begged him to open the front clasp. When he did, she trembled in anticipation. His touch was heaven, but she'd known it would be. They would have been so good together tonight, so very, very good.

Backing her against the car, he thrust one leg between her thighs. Ah, sweet pressure. She bore down against it as his kiss deepened and became more urgent.

She responded to that urgency, rocking against his firm thigh as he massaged her breast and pinched her nipple hard. His tongue thrust rhythmically, filling her mind with images of their naked bodies locked together. The tight coil of an impending climax made her gasp against his plundering mouth. Awash in the fantasy of what they'd hoped for but wouldn't have tonight, she let herself go.

He swallowed her cries and gathered her shuddering body close. When the storm had passed, she sagged against him, weak from the power of her orgasm. Lifting his mouth from hers, he peppered her face with light kisses.

"That's better." His voice was as soft as the touch of his lips. "I didn't want to end this night without giving you something."

She took a shaky breath. "But I didn't give you anything."

"That's where you're wrong." He rubbed the small of her back and gazed down at her. "You let yourself come apart in my arms. I treasure that."

"Not half as much as I do, I'll bet." She looked into his shadowed face. "Look, I know it's a long way from Cheyenne to Sheridan, but—"

"It's getting shorter by the second."

"And I already have a supply of condoms."

"There's that. Wouldn't want them to go to waste."

"So…" She traced the line of his jaw with her finger. "If you'd consider making the drive next weekend, I promise that my parents will not be sleeping in my bed."

"Gonna tell them that I'll be sleeping in it, instead?"

"Not on your life, cowboy. I've learned my lesson on that score. Gonna tell Rosie and Herb you're driving up?"

"Hadn't planned to."

"So you'll do it?"

"Lady, wild horses couldn't keep me away."

8

Ty USED THE drive to the ranch to sober up and tamp down his lust for the woman at the wheel of the Subaru. She'd caught fire so fast tonight that he could imagine how spectacular she'd be under better circumstances. If he allowed himself to think about the way she'd responded to him, he'd only torture himself with what could have been.

So they talked about her folks and her other relatives, of which there seemed to be a bunch living in Cheyenne—both sets of grandparents, aunts and uncles, and cousins galore. After meeting Ellen and Art, Ty could see why Whitney was such a bright spirit. They both had an optimistic outlook and they obviously adored their daughter.

Although they might be a tad overprotective, he couldn't blame them. Until this move to Sheridan, she'd lived in Cheyenne all her life. "Considering your mom only knew me from that calendar," he said, "I'm not surprised they showed up tonight."

"Me, either, but she feels guilty about intruding. I told her not to worry about it. When I called her on Thanksgiving I probably sounded homesick, and then I mentioned I'd invited you over to help decorate the tree. She thought I was going off the deep end and needed an intervention."

"You think she's feeling better about me now?"

"Definitely. Until tonight, she was afraid I'd been seduced by a rogue." Then she laughed. "Good thing she wasn't in the parking lot or she might still think so."

"No kidding. I was a desperate man."

"I'm not complaining." She glanced over at him. "About next weekend, I'll do my best to clear time, but I should warn you that I'll have to work at least part of each day."

"That still leaves us two full nights."

"I know, but it seems inhospitable to go off and leave you alone in my apartment."

"That's okay. I can bring my laptop and work on case files while you're gone. I'd be doing that at home, anyway. I won't have to worry about getting behind."

"Are you okay sneaking into town without telling Rosie and Herb?"

"If you can keep a secret, so can I." He settled back in the seat and turned so he could watch the play of light on her face. It would be a long week, but he was a master at delayed gratification.

"What if you should meet someone you know on the street?"

"Easy. I won't go anywhere. I'll drive straight to your place and stay there until I leave on Sunday."

"Mmm. I like that. It'll be like I have you captive for the weekend."

"A willing captive. Just bring me food and drink and I'll satisfy your every desire."

She squirmed in her seat. "You're turning me on."

"And that cuts both ways."

"Predictable anatomical consequences?"

"Exactly. Let's talk about something that has nothing to do with sex." He had a sudden thought. "Unless you tucked one of the condoms in your purse?"

"Sorry. Didn't occur to me. What if I had?"

"Isn't it obvious?"

"Are you talking about having sex in the boonies?"

"Damn straight. You have the perfect car for it. The backseat folds down. The road between here and the ranch has dozens of little places to pull off into the trees."

"That's right. You went to high school here. You would know about those places, wouldn't you?"

"Yes, ma'am."

She blew out a breath. "And now I'm all hot and bothered again."

"But we have no little raincoat."

"No, and even if we did, that would be a bad idea. We're supposed to go to a party and if we stopped along the way we might never make it. Even if we did finally arrive there, we'd look as if we'd been having sex in the boonies."

"Good point. Although like your folks, everyone at the party will assume that we're attracted to each other, and if we haven't done the deed, we're heading in that direction."

"Which we are."

"In six days." After just congratulating himself on his ability to delay gratification, he saw those six days stretching out endlessly. "When are your parents leaving tomorrow, exactly?"

"I have to go back to work at four, so they'll probably take off around three-thirty. Why?"

"Oh, just thinking."

"I recognize that tone. I work until seven, so don't even go there, Ty. That's crazy."

"I'm not so sure. I could be at your place when you get home. If I left by one in the morning, I'd be back in Cheyenne in time to shower, shave and head off to work."

"Absolutely not. I won't have you cavorting in my bed until the wee hours and then struggling to stay awake on the five-hour drive home."

"Cavorting?" He chuckled. "Is that what we'd be doing?"

"No, because we won't be in my bed together tomorrow tonight and that's final. Get some sleep tonight and drive back to Cheyenne fully rested. We'll reconnect on Friday night whenever you get to town."

"I figure it might be after ten on Friday. You okay with that?"

"Are you kidding? Of course I am. I can't wait."

Nothing like a hot woman eager for his body to make him feel a little reckless. "I could show up at seven-fifteen tomorrow night and stay until nine. Then I'd be home by two. I can operate on five hours of sleep, no problem. I survived on less when I was in law school."

"I swear, Ty Slater, if you're at my apartment tomorrow night, I'll send you packing."

"After we have sex or before? Because I'm okay with you sending be packing afterward."

"We're not having sex tomorrow night, so save yourself the trouble and drive home at a decent hour."

He reached over and stroked her thigh. "Sure about that?"

"Yes!" She slapped his hand. "Cut it out."

Chuckling, he sat back in his seat. He'd heard the telltale quiver in her voice. "Okay, then I'll arrive at seven-fifteen and leave by eight."

"That's almost drive-by sex. I'm not interested."

"Yes, you are. You're breathing a lot faster than you were a few minutes ago. We can make this work, Whitney. Short and extremely sweet. Then I don't have to leave town without knowing what it's like to be deep inside you."

She sucked in a breath. "You're playing dirty."

"Whatever works."

"My mother was right in the first place. You are a rogue."

"Only with you. With everyone else I'm a conservative lawyer with an extremely well-organized sock drawer. You inspire me to be something different. And I like it. I think you like it, too."

"Maybe I do, but please don't stay in town until I get off work tomorrow night. Be sensible and go home."

"Tell you what. I'll sleep on it tonight and decide tomorrow." He already knew what he was going to do, but she'd probably buy that line of BS.

"Good. Once the buzz from the wine has worn off, I'm sure you'll see that waiting until next weekend is the way to go."

"You're probably right. Okay, slow down a little. The turnoff to the ranch is up here to the left."

She eased up on the gas. "I'm really glad to be invited to this party. Ever since I heard about the academy I've wanted to visit."

"You should have asked. Rosie would have been thrilled to have you come out."

"I know, but she's been so busy I didn't want to bother her. It's only recently that I've noticed she's starting to relax. This stamp of approval from the state must have made her very happy."

"It did. They're booked up for the spring semester

even without this, but now the kids will get high school credit. That's huge." They came to the familiar bend in the road. "Next road on your left."

She turned in where he'd indicated and her headlights swept over the sign. "Wow, that's beautiful."

"My foster brother Damon and his fiancée, Philomena, made it."

"Oh, Damon and Phil! They come in for coffee a couple of times a week. Cute couple. And of course I recognized him right away from his calendar picture. Will they both be here?"

"I'm sure."

"Anyone else I might know?"

"Cade Gallagher."

"Right! Mister April, the first boy Rosie brought to the ranch. He doesn't stop by for coffee all that often, but Lexi does. And her mom, Janine, was in the shop just today."

"She and her husband should be there. They've been close friends of Rosie and Herb for years."

"I just realized that I might recognize most everyone here if they buy coffee at Rangeland Roasters."

"If they're friends of Rosie's, chances are they do because she's recommended the place. She's big on supporting local businesses."

"I love Rosie."

"That makes two of us." At his first glimpse of the ranch house, he admired the excellent spacing of the lights strung along the roofline. He and Damon had accomplished that on Thursday morning while Cade had straw-bossed the operation. Cade had plenty of talents, but using hand tools wasn't one of them.

Damon had forbidden Cade to touch the staple gun after he'd fooled around and stapled his sleeve to the porch railing. Cade and Damon had traded insults while Damon had taken his own sweet time pulling out the staple with a pair of pliers. He'd turned it into a major operation, and Ty had laughed until his sides hurt. Good times.

The lights created pools of color in the clean snow banked against the front porch, just as they had years ago when Ty had lived here. Apparently Rosie and Herb had stopped putting them up after all the boys left, but if Damon had anything to say about it, they'd go up every Christmas from now on.

He'd become quite the sentimental guy after getting engaged to Phil. They'd have a late June wedding at the ranch, and Ty already had it on his calendar. Rosie was beside herself with joy because she'd finally get to help plan a wedding for one of her boys.

"The ranch house looks really pretty, Ty. Who put up the lights?"

"Me and Damon."

"He's special to you, isn't he?"

"How can you tell?"

"It's the way you say his name. Was he one of your best friends back then?"

"Not when I was living here, although I always liked the guy. We've become a lot closer recently, but my best friend at the ranch was Brant Ellison."

"That name doesn't sound familiar." She navigated around the snow-packed circular drive. "Where should I park?"

"There's a space between those two trucks."

She pulled the Subaru neatly into the spot. "So will Brant be here?"

"I doubt it. He's working on a ranch down in Cody and last time I talked to him he wasn't planning to drive up this weekend. Something about a mare about to foal."

"Too bad he couldn't come." She shut off the engine. "I'd like to meet your best friend. He probably has some good stories about you."

"Oh, yeah, he does." Ty laughed. "And you can't believe a single one of them."

"So you say."

"He'll probably come up Christmas Eve and stay for a couple of days. Maybe then you could—"

"I'll be in Cheyenne with my folks those exact same days."

"Oh. Well, then we'll just see how things go. Maybe he'll stay a little longer."

"Sure. You never know. It might work out."

"I hope so." All of a sudden he really wanted her to meet Brant. Funny how that hadn't seemed the least bit important with the various women he'd dated since he'd left Thunder Mountain. But Brant would like Whitney and vice versa.

He could almost hear the big guy advising him. *Hang on to this one, kid,* he'd say. *She's a keeper.* Brant was only a year older than Ty, but he was two inches taller and thirty pounds heavier. He'd called Ty kid from day one.

"Thanks for driving us here." Ty unbuckled his seat belt. "I'll stick with coffee so I can take the wheel on the way back. You should have some champagne. I'll bet they'll be serving it."

"You were planning to drive me back? You don't have to do that. I can drive myself home. I'll bet someone could give you a ride in the morning."

"They could, but I'd rather let you enjoy the party."

She gazed at him. "That's very sweet, but I hate that you'll have to turn right around and drive home."

"I'm not crazy about it, either, but it's too cold to sleep

in the truck and your futon is out of the question. I'm not getting a motel…" He paused as a new thought came to him. "Unless you would consider—"

"No, Ty, I would not." Laughter rippled in her voice as she unbuckled her seat belt "Tempting as you are, it would be just my luck the night clerk would be a customer at Rangeland Roasters."

"Hadn't thought of that. Guess I'll be driving back to the ranch." He glanced at her. "Ready to go in?"

"Almost." She reached behind her seat and pulled her purse into her lap. "Let me fix my lipstick first. Someone kissed it all off."

"That rogue from the Thunder Mountain calendar, I'll bet."

"Matter of fact, you're right." She flipped open the lighted visor mirror and he watched her stroke her upper lip with deep red lipstick. It slid smoothly as she applied it to one half of the bow and then the other, leaving her top lip looking wet.

He'd seen the color on her earlier when she'd come out of her bedroom ready for the party, but this was different. He was watching her put it on a mouth that he craved with an intensity that amazed him. Quietly he laid his hat on the dash.

Lips parted, she swept the lower one with the ruby color and inspected the result in the mirror. "Done."

"Afraid not." Tunneling his fingers through her hair, he leaned over and took that glistening mouth with a swiftness that made her gasp. Immediately he eased up on the pressure so he could enjoy the erotic feel of her glossy lips against his. He'd be covered in dark red lipstick but he didn't care. She'd have tissues in her purse. All women did.

But not all women could kiss like Whitney Jones. She

gave up the fight at once, obviously realizing that once his mouth had touched down, her repair job was ruined. So she cupped the back of his head and opened to him with a soft moan that sent a message straight to his groin.

He had no business doing this when they had a party to go to, but her coat was still unzipped from their last hot kiss and he wanted to touch her more than he wanted to breathe. Her front-clasp bra was a temptation he couldn't deny himself.

In seconds he was stroking her silky breasts and listening to the sweet music of her whimpers. He wouldn't take things as far as he had last time. They were right outside his foster parents' house, for God's sake.

But when she sucked on his tongue, he quickly became hard. If he didn't stop now, he was liable to haul her into the backseat, and that would not be cool. He'd started this, so he'd have to put an end to it, much as he didn't want to.

Pulling together the unraveling threads of his self-control, he lifted his head and slowly slipped his hand out from under her sweater. "Enough." His voice sounded like the scrape of a boot on gravel.

She sucked in air. "What was that all about?"

"Your lipstick." Releasing his grip on her head, he reached under her sweater, located the two parts of her bra clasp and fastened it.

"I'm sure you have it from ear to ear, now." She straightened her sweater.

"Probably. But when you started putting it on, I… snapped."

"I noticed." She took a deep breath. "But why? I'm sure you've watched women applying lipstick before."

"Sure, but not when I was out of my mind with sexual frustration."

"Well, congratulations, because now so am I."

"Sorry."

"No, you're not."

He laughed softly. "You're right, I'm not. This has been the most sexually nerve-racking yet exciting few days I've had in a long time. It's comforting to know you're as jacked up as I am."

"You're building a case for coming over at seven-fifteen tomorrow night for a quickie, aren't you?"

"Listen to you, talking like a lawyer."

"You must be rubbing off on me."

"Don't I wish? I'm willing to rub anything you care to offer. I'll tell you how depraved I am. While I was kissing you, I considered whether we should bag this party idea and find one of those secluded spots in the woods. We could have a great time, even without condoms."

"But you obviously changed your mind because we're discussing instead of doing."

"I changed my mind because we need to go inside and join the celebration. And because it's too damned cold to park in the woods. We'd have to leave the motor running and the heater on, which could lead to using up all the gas and getting stranded."

"Sounds like the voice of experience."

"Maybe."

She rummaged in her purse. "Lean over here and let me wipe the lipstick off."

He moved into the light and she began to giggle. "What?"

"You remind me of the time my three-year-old cousin Stuart got ahold of his mom's lipstick."

"Nice. I love being compared to a toddler run amuck. Just wipe it off, please."

"You started it. I was only trying to make myself

presentable and you…pounced." She rubbed at his face with a tissue.

The light from the mirror was bright enough for him to see her face. "You have it all over you, too."

"I don't doubt it. That was freshly applied lipstick and the kind I like isn't smear-proof."

"This one makes your lips look wet."

She rolled her eyes. "I *know* it does. That's why I bought it."

"Aha! Entrapment! No wonder I couldn't resist you."

She finished wiping his face. "Nice try, but I think the responsibility for this kissfest lies with you. Anyway, you're good to go. Let's see what this episode did to… Oh, my God. I look like a deranged circus clown. Remind me never to put on lipstick in your presence again. You can't handle it."

"But you'll have to before we go in there."

"That's right, I will." She dabbed at her mouth with a tissue. "So here's an idea. You stand outside and I'll lock the doors."

"That's crazy."

"No, *you're* crazy. I'm just taking precautions."

He leaned back against his seat and closed his eyes. "Just do it. I won't look."

"Okay, but I'm watching you."

"I promised, and I keep my word. But answer me this." He kept his eyes closed. "Did you like it?"

"You know I did. Just don't do it again in the next five seconds."

"I won't, but I still think we need to get naked before I leave for Cheyenne." He listened to her breathing change and smiled. She thought so, too.

9

WALKING THROUGH THE door of the ranch house, Whitney got quite a reception. Several people sitting around the fire leaped up and came to greet her, including Lexi, who took charge of her coat and purse. Whitney said hello to Janine and met her husband, Aaron.

Damon and Phil each gave her a hug, and then Rosie hurried in from the kitchen, wiping her hands on a towel and beaming with happiness.

"I'm so glad you could come." She tossed the towel over her shoulder and grasped Whitney's hands in both of hers.

"Thank you for inviting me."

"Should have thought of it sooner. I wish it wasn't so dark and cold so we could show you around the place. You'll have to come back. Anytime is fine. You don't have to wait for Ty to bring you."

"I'd love to."

"Then it's settled. Excuse me for a minute. I have to go grab a couple more bottles of champagne. Now that you're here, we can do the official toast."

"You were waiting for us?" Whitney was touched.

"Of course!"

As Rosie hurried off, Whitney thanked her lucky stars that she'd made the decision to come out here.

"You should definitely visit again soon." Phil, her red hair piled on top of her head, linked her arm through Damon's. "Before you leave, I'll give you my cell number so you can let me know when you're coming out. I love giving tours of the cabins."

"For a good reason." Damon gestured toward his fiancée. "She designed these great loft beds. They're basically a bunk bed without the bottom bunk so a desk and dresser can fit underneath. They're super cool."

"I'll vouch for that." Cade walked over with a champagne flute in each hand and mischief in his green eyes. He handed one each to Whitney and Ty. "It's a darned lucky thing I'm on the job getting Whitney champagne, Slater, or the poor woman would die of thirst."

"I notice they're only about half full, bro."

"Patience, grasshopper. More's on the way."

"I'm on it!" A man in his sixties standing behind a makeshift bar in the corner popped the cork on a bottle of bubbly. Herb had only been in Rangeland Roasters a couple of times, but Whitney recognized him because he'd always come in with Rosie.

Cade turned to Whitney. "Your coffee is great, at least the few times I've managed to get there."

"Thank you."

"But I have to question your taste in men. What're you doing with this bum?"

She laughed. "He's my ticket into this private party. A girl has to do what a girl has to do."

Ty lifted his eyebrows and she grinned at him before taking a sip of her champagne.

"You make a good point," Cade said. "The guest list

is pretty darned exclusive. But now that you're here, feel free to ditch him."

Ty rolled his eyes. "Says the loser who can't handle a staple gun without stapling his sleeve to the porch railing."

"Oh?" Whitney glanced at Cade.

"I have no idea what he's talking about. Oh, look. Here comes Dad with more champagne."

"Welcome to Thunder Mountain Ranch," Herb said as walked toward her.

"And also Thunder Mountain Academy, which I understand is now accredited." Whitney smiled at him. "Congratulations."

"We're tickled about it. Molly Radcliffe is in charge of the curriculum and she's over the moon. Molly and Ben are visiting her family in Arizona, but they're here in spirit."

"Oh, I know them. She teaches at the community college and he's the saddlemaker."

"Yep. He helped design the logo and that sign out front. Then Phil and Damon made it. We have some talented folks around here. But I'm not doing my job. I'm supposed to be pouring champagne. Let me top off your glass." He filled it almost to the brim before motioning to Ty. "How about you?"

"I'm good with what I have here. I'm driving Whitney back to town."

"Not in the next five minutes, I hope."

"No."

"That's good." Herb eyed Ty's glass. "I guess you have enough for a decent swallow. Don't want any wimpy toasting going on tonight."

"That's for sure." Cade surveyed the room. "Now if I just could remember where I put my glass, I'd be a happy man. Don't want to dirty up another one, seeing as how Damon will be the poor slob who has to wash them all after the party. I'd hate for him to get dishpan hands on my account."

"This would be your glass, cowboy, and I even filled it for you." Lexi joined the group and handed him one of the flutes she was carrying.

"Ah, thank you, Lex." He wrapped an arm around her shoulders. "Don't know what I'd do without you."

"I do," Damon said. "You'd revert to being the sorry mess you were before she came along."

Cade lifted his glass in Damon's direction. "That would be a pot-and-kettle statement right there, bro. We all remember the sad state you were in before Phil took you on."

"Can't argue with you there. We're both a couple of lucky dogs."

Cade nodded. "That's a fact."

"I'm loving this conversation." Lexi looked over at Phil. "How about you?"

"Oh, yeah. Maybe we should give them champagne more often."

From across the room, Rosie tapped on the side of her glass to get everyone's attention. "Looks as if we all have champagne." She glanced around. "Many of you in this room helped make Thunder Mountain Academy come to life, but there are some who couldn't make it here tonight. I raise my glass to all of you and anyone not present. Herb and I love you all and we're so…" She swallowed and looked at Herb.

"We're so grateful," he finished in a husky voice, putting his arm around Rosie. "So very grateful."

For a split second the room was silent, and in that moment, Whitney understood what an emotional impact this project had on everyone—Rosie, Herb, the foster brothers and everyone who had been a part of this ranch for years.

Then cheers and whistles erupted and they all lifted their glasses and drank. Whitney promised herself that she'd drive out here next week, tour the facility and see if there was anything she could do to help.

She'd gathered from Rosie's stray comments that without Thunder Mountain Academy, she and Herb might have been forced to sell the ranch. Whitney wasn't clear on the reason for that and she'd ask Ty on the way home. She'd just thought it was a good idea that needed to happen. She hadn't realized the implications for Rosie and Herb if it hadn't become a reality.

She didn't know exactly how she could help other than her degree and a general knowledge of running a business. Rosie and Herb probably had all the advice they needed, but if not, she'd make herself available. Rangeland Roasters had taught her quite a bit and she'd be happy to share.

After the toast, the party kicked into high gear. Rosie hauled out an ancient stereo and a few country CDs while the men moved the furniture to the edges of the room. Rugs were rolled and tucked away. Apparently she and Ty would end up dancing, after all.

Lexi and Cade started it off, but before long Ty pulled her out on the makeshift dance floor.

"What if I can't dance?"

"Too late." With a grin, he spun her around and they were off.

Fortunately she could dance, although not as well as Ty. But she'd been an athlete all her life—volleyball, tennis and skiing. Dancing was simply another form of athletic movement, right? Or maybe not. With a partner like Ty, dancing was foreplay.

Until now, she hadn't understood the erotic nuances of a two-step. He created just enough bodily contact to drive her crazy, but not enough to satisfy her craving for his touch. Maybe a slow dance would come along, but no. This was a celebration and everyone wanted movement and laughter.

She loved the energy in the room. This was her kind of celebration, although she'd never attended such a party with a man as sexy as Ty. The more champagne she drank, the better she danced. The better she danced, the more she lusted after her tall dance partner. By the time he drew her aside and suggested they might want to head back, she had a good buzz going and was thinking how nice a round of hot sweaty sex would feel.

They retrieved their coats and her purse. She said goodbye to everyone, which included plenty of hugs and promises to get together again soon. She'd made more friends in one night than in five months of living in Sheridan.

Once out on the porch, she sucked in the cold air and told herself to settle down. She wouldn't be having sex with Ty, no matter how seductively he danced. Digging in her purse, she eventually found her keys and handed them over. "Great party."

"Rosie and Herb always throw great parties." He looped an arm over her shoulders as they walked across the crusty snow to the car.

"Does everyone usually dance?"

"Not so much. If you really want to know, I think Rosie engineered that because she wanted us to dance together."

"You're kidding."

"I'm not. She wants us to become a couple and she's proud of the way I dance. She's hoping you'll be swept away, so to speak."

"I am."

"You are?" He clicked the remote and the Subaru's taillights flashed. "You're not joking?"

"Dancing with you has turned me on like you wouldn't believe."

"Hm. Good to know." He opened the passenger door. "In you go."

"No, it's not good to know." She gazed up at him as he stood beside the open door. "We're no better off now than we were before. This is an impossible situation. Between my folks and this party, we're SOL."

"Maybe not." He closed the door and walked around to climb into the driver's seat.

"Yes, we are, Ty. So just take me home so I can sleep alone in misery on my cute but uncomfortable futon."

His low chuckle was the sexiest sound in the world.

"Go ahead and laugh, but it's not funny."

"No, but it's not as hopeless as you think, either." He started the car and backed out of the parking space. "While you were drinking champagne, I was drinking coffee and my brain started working again. I came up with an idea."

"What sort of idea?" He looked all cowboyish in his hat and shearling coat as he expertly navigated the winding road. She was ready to listen to anything, no matter how ridiculous it sounded. She wanted the hands gripping the steering wheel to be gripping her, instead, while he stroked deep, and not with his tongue, either.

"It's not a perfect idea, but…" He glanced down at the gauges. "I think you have enough gas in the tank to make it work."

"Make what work? Where are we going?"

"Back to Sheridan." He turned onto the main road and accelerated.

"Then what?"

He glanced at her. "Like I said, it's not a great plan."

"Any plan is better than no plan."

His little smile indicated he liked that response. "Okay, I have to ask at this point, are you rethinking having me come over tomorrow at seven-fifteen?"

"*Yes*. Are you happy, now?"

"Very happy. I was planning to show up, anyway, but this gives me the green light."

"I wouldn't call it the green light. I would call it the yellow caution light. I may want you, but I still think having you stay longer in Sheridan is a bad idea."

"Let me be the judge of that."

She studied him, and what a fun exercise that was. He looked determined and sure, as if he knew exactly what he wanted and how to go about getting it. Maybe it was the champagne talking, but she was inclined to let him work this out. "So what's this new plan of yours?"

He hesitated. "Now that I'm coming over tomorrow night for sure, maybe we should skip it."

"That depends. Does it result in us having sex tonight?"

"Yes."

"The whole enchilada kind of sex?"

He laughed. "Interesting choice of words, but yes."

"No, no, not enchiladas." She remembered the chopstick incident and giggled. "Too limp."

"Trust me, that won't be a problem."

"The whole taquito. How about that?" She couldn't seem to stop giggling. "No, wait, they're kinda small."

He snorted.

"Aren't you going to tell me that won't be a problem, either?"

"I will not."

"Come on, don't be shy. Unless you've been stuffing a sock in your pants, you're no taquito."

"Whitney Jones, how you talk! I think you're toasted."

"I do believe I am. Now tell me what I can expect once you unveil that bad boy of yours. Are we talking taquito or chimichanga?"

He grinned. "You're pretty funny when you're smashed."

"You're avoiding the question."

"Give it up. I'm not telling you."

"Why not?"

"Ever hear the expression *all hat and no cattle*?"

"No, but we're not discussing hats and cattle. We're discussing your—"

"True cowboys don't boast, not about the size of their spread or the size of, well, anything."

She took some time to consider that. The implication warmed all her lady parts.

"But I will tell you I'm not stuffing a sock in my pants."

"All righty, then." She took a shaky breath. "Now that we've settled that matter, what's this plan you keep not telling me about?"

"We head back to the parking lot, and assuming you're not fast asleep by then, I grab the box of condoms I left in my truck and we put the seat back down in your Subaru."

"You have a box of condoms in your truck?"

"That's where the four I left at your place are from. I didn't want to bring in the whole box. That seemed excessive."

She laughed. "What about me? I put a whole box in my bedside table drawer."

"It's your place. You can have six boxes if you want but I didn't want to make assumptions."

"You are such a gentleman."

"I keep trying to convince you I'm not. A gentleman wouldn't invite you to have sex in the back of your own car in the middle of a cold Wyoming night while using your gas to keep the heater going."

"Guess not." She smiled. "That smacks of desperation."

"I know, and if you want to veto the—"

"And I'm so desperate. Let's do it."

Ty tugged on the brim of his hat and nudged the speedometer up another notch. "Hot damn."

10

Ty had no wish to pick up a speeding ticket, but every time he looked at the needle, he was at least ten miles over and he had to force himself to ease up on the pedal. Excitement surged through him. They'd stopped talking, as if words would break the spell that anticipation had created.

He made it to her parking lot in far less time than prudent driving would have required, but he was a man on fire. Pulling into her numbered spot, he put the car in Park and left the motor running. "Be right back." His voice sounded hoarse. It was a wonder he could talk at all, the way his heart was racing.

His hand shook as he unlocked his truck and reached for the latch on the console compartment. The latch resisted, and he swore. *Take it easy, Slater. Don't jam it or you'll be one sorry SOB.*

Stepping back, he took a deep breath. Then he tried again, and the latch popped open. The box of condoms was cold to the touch, and he wondered if the condoms would be cold, too. Wouldn't matter for long. He shoved the box in his coat pocket and locked his truck.

He couldn't remember ever wanting a woman so

much that he turned into fumblefingers. He hoped putting down the backseat wouldn't be too tricky because he was trembling as if he had a fever. Which in a way, he did.

Hurrying back to the car, he unbuttoned his coat. Even the sudden chill didn't cool him off. As he opened the driver's side door, warm air spilled out and the dome light came on. Apparently he wouldn't have to worry about putting down the backseat. She'd already done it.

Even more amazing, she'd come up with a blanket and spread it across the upholstered surface. Her coat lay crumpled on the front passenger seat and she sat in back taking off her shoes. She looked up and smiled. "You might want to come in through the side door." Then she tossed her shoe into the front seat and began taking off the other one.

He passed her the condom box, ditched his coat and hat, then crawled in through the side door.

He'd moved fast, but that didn't explain why he was having trouble breathing. No, that was all Whitney's fault. She was wiggling out of her jeans. He sat immobilized as she revealed creamy thighs and shapely calves. And her panties were bright pink.

Then the dome light clicked off and everything went back to shades of gray. He tugged off his boots and unsnapped his cuffs as she threw her jeans in the front. His eyes had adjusted enough that he could tell she was pulling her sweater over her head. He'd bet her bra was bright pink, too. He didn't want muted gray and indistinct shadows, damn it.

The sweater went sailing in the same direction as her other clothes. Then she came toward him on her hands and knees. "Need help, cowboy?"

"Just light." His shirt snaps popped as he wrenched

it open. "I didn't think about us being in the dark. God, but I want to see you!"

"Can't help you there." She knelt in front of him, her breathing shallow. "But you can touch me in the dark." And she unhooked the front of her bra.

He sucked in a breath. Even in the weak light, he could tell that she was magnificent, worthy of being sculpted by a master. Reaching out, he slid the straps of her bra free and it fell to the blanket.

"I can almost see you," he murmured. "Tomorrow night I will, but for now…" He cradled a warm breast in each hand and she shivered. "Cold?" He stroked his thumbs over her taut nipples.

"Excited. You really know how to touch a girl so she feels special."

"You are special." He kneaded her full breasts. "I love touching you like this, even if…"

"If what?"

"If the more I do it, the harder I get."

"Then do you want to—"

"Nope. Let me play."

She swallowed. "You're very good at playing."

"Glad you think so."

"I've spent the past ten miles dreaming of you…playing." She covered his hands with hers, lifting her breasts as she leaned toward him. "And kissing me…here."

With a groan, he dipped his head and placed rapid, openmouthed kisses all over her silken breasts. As her breathing quickened, he used his tongue to lick and tease his way to one pert nipple. He circled it slowly once and then once again before nibbling gently with his teeth. At last he drew it into his mouth and began to suck.

Moaning, she arched her back and clutched his head. He hollowed his cheeks and pulled her in deep as he massaged her breasts with both hands. Heat simmered in his groin, pulsing in his rigid cock and aching balls.

Not yet. Not yet. He feasted on her other breast until she quivered and dug her fingertips into his scalp. When she began to pant, he absorbed the wonder of what was happening. Just this, only this, and he could make her come. He tugged more rhythmically on her breast.

She gasped. "Oh, Ty... *Ty*." She tensed, and then she let go, abandoning herself to her climax with a soft cry.

He wrapped her in his arms and buried his face against her full breasts as she shuddered in the aftermath of her orgasm. What a miracle she was. And he was the lucky guy holding her tonight.

As she quieted, she stroked his hair. "I love coming that way. But if a guy can't wait..."

"I can." Barely. If he had to wait much longer, his zipper might self-destruct.

"Thank you for that." She leaned away from him. "But let's get you out of those jeans."

"Let's do."

She laughed. "You sound pretty eager."

"Lady, you have no idea."

"Then lie down and I'll help you."

"That could be fun." He stretched out on the blanket as much as he could. Even with the seat down, he didn't quite fit, lengthwise. He wasn't complaining. Whitney had already unbuckled his belt and unfastened the top button of his jeans.

"I'm going to do this gradually." She eased down the zipper of his fly. "You're really smooshed in there and I don't want to cause any damage."

"I'm tougher than you think." But he clenched his jaw at the sweet torture of having her release him from bondage.

"Are you?" She stroked a finger along the ridge of his cock. Even through the cotton briefs, she left a trail of sparks.

He gasped. "I take it back. I'm not tough at all. One more of those and I'll fold. Move back, lady. This is a man's job."

Laughing, she scooted away as he peeled off his jeans and his briefs. While he was at it, he pulled off his socks. Then he sat up and shrugged out of his shirt.

He turned to her. "There's the little matter of those hot pink panties."

"These hot pink panties?" She twirled them on the end of her finger, teasing him with the scent of an aroused woman.

"Yeah, those." He grabbed them and rubbed the damp silk between his fingers. "The ones that let me know how much you want me."

"If you want to know that, just ask me."

"All right." Setting the panties aside, he eased down beside her. Then he wrapped an arm around her waist and pulled her in close. "How much do you want me, Whitney?"

She flattened her palm against his back and inched closer. "Enough to have sex with you in the back of my car in the middle of a Wyoming winter night."

His heart thundered. "Then I guess that's what we need to do."

"I'm counting on it."

Using the tips of his fingers, he located her mouth in the dark so he could give her a quick kiss. "Don't move. I have to suit up." As he rolled over and located the box, he could hear her giggling. "What?" He opened the box and took out a packet. "What's so funny?"

"You telling me you have to *suit up*. I'm picturing you

zipping yourself into some kind of space suit so you can blast off to Mars."

He put on the condom and turned back to her. "That's exactly what I have in mind."

"You do?"

"Yeah. Come over here." He guided her into position until she was lying beneath him. "Let's launch this rocket."

"You're crazy."

"Go crazy with me, Whitney." After grabbing those wet panties, he knew she was ready. Her heat called to him as he settled himself between her thighs and nudged her slick entrance with the tip of his cock.

She wound her arms around his neck. "I guess craziness is what I signed on for." She might sound casual about it, but her body quivered with each breath.

"You can still change your mind. It's not too late now, but in another second it will be."

"Ty Slater, are you stalling?"

Maybe. And not because he didn't want her with every fiber of his being. But underneath that physical craving that pushed him to take her with gusto, he heard a voice of caution that told him this moment could change his life forever. He ignored it. "Only a fool would do that." And he plunged deep.

The instant he did, he knew the truth of it. His life had changed forever. She rose to meet him and welcomed him in a way that he'd never felt before. Sinking into her body was like coming home.

In this unlikely place, an apartment complex parking lot, he'd found what he hadn't admitted he'd been searching for with every woman he'd taken to bed. Each rhythmic stroke strengthened the connection as it bathed him in the warmth and light that spilled from Whitney's soul.

He savored the wonder of being inside her as if he'd crawled through a barren desert and stumbled upon an oasis. Again and again he thrust deep, glorying in the richness that he found within the moist recesses of her body. His climax hovered near, demanding to be satisfied, and he kept pushing it away. He wasn't ready for this to end.

Instead, he reveled in her responsiveness. With a slight shift here, a faster pace there, he coaxed another orgasm from her. And another. She was so easy to please and he could think of nothing he'd rather do than give her pleasure.

Then she wrapped her legs around his waist and cupped his face in both hands. Her brown eyes were dark with passion and purpose as she looked up at him. "Your turn," she murmured.

"But I like—"

"Your turn." And she drew him in close and worked her magic as she held his gaze.

Locked in tight, he could barely move as she rocked slowly against him. The sweet undulations of her body gradually eroded his control. He felt himself slipping, slipping, until all the restraints gave way and he came in a rush, crying out at the intensity of an orgasm that went on…and on…and on.

When the waves of sensation began to ebb, he rested his forehead on her shoulder and wondered what the hell he was going to do now. She'd just given him the most significant sexual encounter of his life. It had been so perfect that it scared him to death.

He was used to having good sex with the women he'd dated. But no matter how much he'd enjoyed those relationships, giving them up hadn't been a problem when they'd ended for one reason or another. He was in completely different territory, now.

Before this he'd thought the term *making love* was a euphemism. He'd used it often himself because it sounded nicer, more considerate. But making love had nothing to do with being nice or considerate. He knew that now. Making love had the power to transform physical pleasure into a life-changing, transcendent experience.

Already he wanted her again because she'd take him to that place where nothing mattered but the joy of right now. But asking for more would be selfish. She had work in the morning and her parents to entertain. She needed gas to get to work and they were using it up the longer they stayed here with the motor running.

He dragged in a breath. "I don't want to move, but we need to."

"I know." Her arms tightened around him. "I don't want to move, either."

Lifting his head, he gazed down at her. He wanted to look into her eyes, but her face was in deep shadow. "I...that was really great." So lame. Really great didn't begin to cover the beauty of what they'd shared, but he doubted he could talk about that without sounding even more idiotic. He wasn't sure he *wanted* to talk about it. The feelings were too tender and new.

"Yes." There was a smile in her voice. "Really great. You've thoroughly convinced me that you should stop by tomorrow night."

"Good. I'll be in the parking lot. I'll watch for your car."

"I would try to get off early, but I just did that tonight, and I can't make a habit of asking people to cover for me. Sets a bad example."

"Agreed." He sighed. "I really don't want to let go of you."

"Lean down here. Let me have one more kiss before we untangle ourselves."

"You bet." They bumped noses and were both laughing by the time he located her mouth. But once he did, once he slipped his tongue inside and deepened the kiss, the magic began all over again. Kissing her had been wonderful before, but now that he'd felt the welcome of her body, a kiss meant so much more. They'd crossed a threshold and he'd remember the joy of loving her for as long as he walked this earth.

With great reluctance he ended the kiss and unwillingly eased away from her warmth. He found his jeans and used the handkerchief in his back pocket to take care of the condom. Then they fumbled around locating their clothes.

He finally got his briefs and jeans back on, but not without a few muttered swearwords. "Much as I loved how tonight turned out, let's not do this again, okay?"

"Yeah, let's not. Ow!"

"What happened?"

"I couldn't find my panties, so I decided to put my jeans on without them. Not a good idea."

"Let me guess. Something silky and blond got caught in the zipper."

"Spoken like someone who's tried the same stunt."

"Once. That was enough."

"Once is enough for me."

"Want me to kiss it and make it better?"

"Yes, but I don't have enough gas in the tank for what would happen after that." She grabbed her sweater from the front seat and pulled it over her head.

"I know. I just checked the gauge. We need to move

it." He patted the area around him and found her panties. "This is no help now, but here."

"Thanks. I'll just put them in the pocket of my coat."

"And here's your bra, too."

"That can go in the other pocket."

"Is it hot pink, too?"

"The bra matches. It's one of my indulgences. I have a whole rainbow of matching bras and panties. Makes me happy."

"Makes me hot."

"Oh, yeah? What's your favorite color?"

"Red."

"Then red it is tomorrow night."

He groaned. "Which now seems like an eternity away." He fastened the snaps on his shirt. "Just know I'll be thinking of your red underwear all day tomorrow."

"Just know that I'll be thinking of you taking them off."

Instead of tucking his shirttails in, he crawled toward her. "I'm coming over there for one more kiss."

She stopped putting on her shoes. Rising to her knees, she took his face in both hands and gave him a hot, openmouthed kiss that made him forget everything but kissing her back. In seconds he'd cupped her delicious bottom and hauled her against his growing erection.

She pressed closer and moaned deep in her throat. That was all the encouragement he needed to slide his hands under her sweater. Leaning back, she gave him access and he took full advantage of the opportunity to caress and knead her plump breasts. His cock strained against his fly.

The kiss grew hotter and their breathing roughened. But when he reached for the button of her jeans, she wrenched her mouth from his. "We have to stop."

He struggled to catch his breath. "I know. I just—"

"Me, too. But we can't."

Slowly he relaxed his fingers and pulled his hands out from under her sweater. "I feel as if we could spend all day in bed and I'd never get tired of touching you, kissing you, thrusting my cock into your—"

She slapped a hand over his mouth. "Stop it. I'm on the verge of an orgasm as it is."

"Want one more for the road?" He reached for the button on her jeans again.

"No." She caught his hand. "I'm not taking any chances on unzipping these jeans."

He sighed and moved away from her. "Okay. Putting on my boots now. Then I'll go turn off the engine. That should motivate us to get the heck out of here."

"It will. Good idea."

Moments later they'd bundled up in their coats and snapped the seat back into place. After he folded the blanket, Whitney tucked it in a zippered bag that went under the seat.

"That came in handy." He'd had the unwelcome thought that she'd set up everything quickly as if she'd done it before. But he wasn't going to ask. If she had, he didn't want to know.

"It's smart to keep a blanket in the car during the winter." She used the remote to lock the doors.

"Yep, sure is." He put his arm around her shoulders as he walked her toward the apartment building.

"Fortunately I've never been stranded where I had to use it to keep warm. So I use it for my nieces and nephews. They love playing in the back of my car whenever the whole family goes on a picnic."

"You know, I hadn't thought of that. I'll bet it would be fun for kids."

"You were afraid I'd had sex with someone else back there, weren't you?"

"Not exactly."

"You were!" She chuckled. "I could hear it in your voice."

"Okay, maybe I did wonder. You put that whole deal together really fast. But even if you had, so what? It's not like we're a couple of untouched virgins."

"No." Their footsteps crunched on the hard-packed snow. "But tonight felt different, sort of like I wish my first time had been."

He was startled by her openness. That was a good description of how he'd felt, too, but he wouldn't have dared say something that vulnerable.

"Only speaking for myself, of course," she added. "Well, here we are. I'm not going to kiss you good-night at the door because our lips might freeze together."

He smiled. "I doubt it. Our kisses are too hot."

"Probably. But let's not chance it."

"Okay, but mostly because it'll just get us both worked up again with no hope of follow-through."

"There's that."

Putting his hands on her shoulders, he looked into her eyes. "Just so you know, I felt the same way."

Her gaze warmed. "Thank you. It's nice to know I wasn't the only one."

"You weren't." He gave her shoulders a squeeze. "Good night, Whitney."

"Good night, Ty. Drive carefully."

"I will."

"I mean it. Don't speed like you did on the way here."

"I won't. Now go in before you get frostbite." He watched until the door closed after her before he walked back to his truck. He would drive carefully. He could

use the time to think about what was happening between them.

He couldn't deny it was the most intense relationship
he'd ever had. And the best one. Physically they were a
perfect fit. Mentally he wasn't so sure. She'd come from
a big, rambunctious, normal family and she obviously
loved talking about them. His past was a lot more complicated and he never talked about the years before his
folks had died.

Maybe they could skate right over that issue and start
a new chapter in the here and now. He hoped so, because
he'd buried most of his childhood memories along with
his parents and he planned to keep it that way.

11

Whitney sat across the booth from her parents while they all had lunch at the same diner where she and Ty had eaten mac and cheese the night before. In her mind, that meal could have taken place in another century. So much had changed since then.

"I'm glad the party was fun." Her mother hadn't asked any pointed questions about Ty, but those could still be coming. "It must have run late. I got up around one and you hadn't come home yet."

"I hope you weren't worried." Wow. Shades of her teen years when she'd had a curfew.

"No, no." But the way her mother said it was a dead giveaway that she *had* been worried.

Whitney battled guilt she had no logical reason to feel. Her parents had chosen to come to her place, which meant she was in charge, not them. Still, she didn't like the idea that her mother had suffered some anxiety because she hadn't come home at what Ellen considered a normal hour.

Actually, she had been home at a normal hour. She just hadn't been upstairs tucked under the covers on her

FREE Merchandise is 'in the Cards' for you!

Dear Reader,

We're giving away FREE MERCHANDISE!

Seriously, we'd like to reward you for reading this novel by giving you **FREE MERCHANDISE** worth over **$20**. And no purchase is necessary!

You see the Jack of Hearts sticker above? Paste that sticker in the box on the Free Merchandise Voucher inside. Return the Voucher promptly...and we'll send you valuable Free Merchandise!

Thanks again for reading one of our novels—and enjoy your Free Merchandise with our compliments!

Pam Powers

Pam Powers

P.S. Look inside to see what Free Merchandise is **"in the cards"** for you!

We'd like to send you two free books like the one you are enjoying now. Your two books have a combined price of over $10, but they are yours to keep absolutely FREE! We'll even send you 2 wonderful surprise gifts. You can't lose!

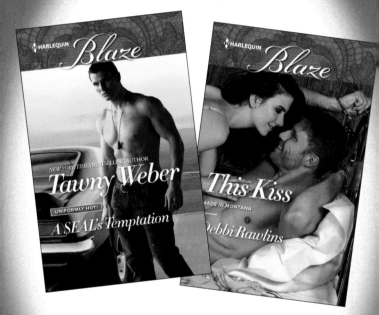

REMEMBER: Your Free Merchandise, consisting of **2 Free Books** and **2 Free Gifts**, is worth over $20.00! No purchase is necessary, so please send for your Free Merchandise today.

Get TWO FREE GIFTS!
We'll also send you two wonderful FREE GIFTS (worth about $10), in addition to your 2 Free books!

Visit us at:
www.ReaderService.com

YOUR FREE MERCHANDISE INCLUDES...

2 FREE Books **AND** 2 FREE Mystery Gifts

futon. And she'd slept like a rock after all those orgasms. *Thank you, Ty.*

"It's hard to turn off that kind of concern," her dad said. "We both try, but it isn't easy."

"I know." Whitney gazed at them. "Well, I don't *know* because I've never had kids, but I can imagine. Ty drank coffee at the party so he drove us home."

Her mother dabbed at her mouth with a napkin. "He seems like a conscientious guy."

"I liked him." Pushing back his plate, her dad reached for the dessert menu propped in the middle of the table. "Seems intelligent and focused on his career. Considering what he had to deal with when he was young, that's admirable." He glanced over the menu. "The cheesecake sounds good. You two going to join me?"

Ellen waved her hands. "Not me. As it is, I'll have to wait a few days before I dare get on the scale. You go ahead, Mr. High Metabolism. Knock yourself out."

"I'll have some with you, Dad." Whitney had inherited his height and his ability to burn calories. She was grateful for both.

"Figured I could count on you, Peanut." He still called her that even though she was five-nine, a college graduate and manager of a flourishing coffee shop. She didn't mind.

"It's a shame Ty doesn't live in Sheridan," Ellen said. "Then you could see more of each other."

"That's the way it goes." She wasn't about to announce that Ty planned to keep the road busy between here and Cheyenne.

Her dad leaned back against the booth. "Well, maybe you two can meet up when you come home for Christmas."

"I think he'll be up here for Christmas."

"Oh." Her dad seemed to consider that. "Makes sense." He shrugged, obviously dismissing the idea that she'd get serious about Ty. "Oh, well."

Her mother, on the other hand, didn't appear to be making that assumption. "So you won't be seeing each other at all? He seemed so taken with you."

"We've talked about finding opportunities to see each other." She thought.

Her mother obviously saw through that vague statement. "I thought so. A man doesn't look at a woman the way he looked at you and then give up because she's a five-hour drive away."

"Mom, we're just getting acquainted. Don't go thinking it's serious."

"I won't." Her mother's tone was breezy and offhand, but her gaze was not. "I did notice the way you looked at him, though."

Whitney's cheeks grew warm. Couldn't put anything past her mother. "I admit he's attractive."

"He's extremely handsome and you know it. When he's wearing that sheepskin coat and a cowboy hat, he could be one of the models in a Western wear magazine. Don't you think so, Art?"

"Leave me out of this. All I can say is that the guy's sharp, dedicated to his career and knows his football. I'm not offering an opinion on how he looks. That's not my area."

Ellen smiled. "We've embarrassed your father."

"Damn straight." He cleared his throat. "I'm not supposed to be thinking about my daughter becoming involved with a man. That kind of image is what causes fathers to oil up their shotguns."

Whitney started laughing. The idea of her quiet, civilized dad pointing a shotgun at someone cracked her up. "You don't even own a shotgun. How can you oil it?"

"Much more of this discussion about Ty's physical attributes and I might be motivated to buy one."

"We'll shut up." She reached across the table and squeezed his arm.

"Thank God. I was about to head over to the counter, order a beer and watch football on the flat screen so you ladies could talk about things I'd rather not hear."

"We can drop the subject of Ty altogether," her mother said, "except I did want to ask one thing. Have you told him about Selena?"

"No. Did you?"

"No, honey. We'd just met the man. That's not the time to be hauling out that kind of information. I just wondered if you'd gotten around to it. You know, in case it turns out we see him again sometime."

"I haven't said anything yet. It's the sort of thing you don't want to blurt out when you first get to know someone."

"I have to know someone really well before I talk about Selena," her dad said. "Fortunately most of my friends were around when she died and they know everything. But new people? Sometimes I don't say a word, ever."

"No reason to." Whitney gazed at her parents, who had been through so much. "I feel the same way. I'm just getting to know Ty, so at what point do you say *Oh, by the way, my twin sister died in a car accident when we were sixteen*. There's never a good time to say that."

"But it's part of who you are," her mother said. "So if he stays in the picture, he needs to know."

"That's a big *if*. We get along great, but we haven't spent all that much time together. Besides, he had a really bad thing happen to him when he was a teenager. I gather he's still dealing with losing his folks, although he pretends he's over it."

Ellen shook her head. "So typical for someone his age. Eventually he'll learn that you don't get over it. You learn to live with it."

"You've both taught me that, but I don't know if he's reached that point. So I…well, I'm not rushing into confiding in him about Selena. That's all I'm saying."

"I think that's wise." Her dad glanced up as the waitress approached. "We'll have two pieces of cheesecake, please. One for me and one for my daughter." He looked over at his wife. "Unless you've changed your mind?"

"Oh, all right. I'll be miserable watching you two eat it, so make that three pieces, please."

Her dad wrapped his arm around his wife and gave her a hug. "Tell you what. I'll go out walking with you every day this week so you can get back to where you want to be."

She smiled at him. "Thanks, Art."

"Anything for my best girl."

Whitney watched them with fondness. Their marriage wasn't perfect because no marriage ever was, but they'd weathered the death of a child and still loved and respected each other. She admired the way they'd come through that crisis together, and if anything, their relationship was stronger as a result.

They ate cheesecake and drank coffee while they discussed the extended family living in Cheyenne. Whitney got caught up on all the gossip—which cousins were doing well and which ones were giving their parents gray hair. One uncle had dealt with a heart problem but he was recovering nicely. All four grandparents were amazingly healthy and enjoying life.

She missed being there to get the information first-hand, but she wouldn't trade her position at Rangeland Roasters for a chance to stay in Cheyenne. Making the break had proven to her that she could survive on her own and find new friends. No matter what happened between her and Ty, she was thriving here.

She saw them off with a mixture of emotions. Her inner child longed to hop in her parents' car and return to her former life in Cheyenne. But the stronger part, the one that had propelled her here to Sheridan, watched them leave with a sigh of relief. She was on her own again. And Ty would be coming over tonight.

Business was brisk at the coffee shop that afternoon, thank God. Whitney needed the distraction to keep her from thinking about Ty's impending arrival at her apartment. She worked right alongside her employees to keep up with the orders.

Shoppers crowded Main Street until well after six, and a good percentage of them stopped in for a cup of coffee and a pastry. The shop had a festive air with everyone carrying bags and boxes filled with Christmas presents and extra decorations. More than one customer mentioned being grateful Rangeland Roasters had come to town.

When Damon and Phil showed up, Whitney greeted them with a big smile. They were more than just customers, now. "Out shopping?" She rang up their order as Meryl started their drinks.

Damon held up a couple of red-and-green shopping bags. "Thought we'd get an early start."

"My dad and stepmom are spending Christmas Eve and Christmas Day with us." Phil pulled money out of her purse.

"Hey, I've got it." Damon put down the bags and reached for his wallet.

"Nope. You paid last time. Remember? We talked about this."

"So we did." Damon chuckled as he tucked his wallet away. "Old habits die hard."

Whitney envied them. They obviously both adored and respected each other. She'd love to have that kind of mutuality with a man someday. She could imagine developing it with Ty, but it was early days, yet.

"Anyway," Phil said, "if you'll be around when my folks are here, I'd love to have you meet them."

"I'd love that, too, but I'm driving down to Cheyenne on Christmas Eve and staying for a couple of days." She handed Phil her change. "We're closing the shop early that day and all day on Christmas."

"As well you should. That's okay. You'll meet them at the wedding, if not before. That reminds me. Text me your address so I can add you to the guest list."

"You're inviting me?"

"Of course." Phil grinned. "We linked arms and drank champagne last night. We're bonded."

"That's right, we did. I had such a good time."

"We all did," Damon said. "It was great having Ty here. I could tell he didn't want to leave today. He was still hanging around the ranch when we left. He may be gone by now, though."

Whitney glanced at the wall clock. Almost six-thirty. "Probably."

"I'll bet he'll stop to say goodbye before he leaves town." Phil's tone was casual as she picked up their two cups of coffee, but there was a knowing twinkle in her blue eyes.

"That would be nice." Whitney's cheeks warmed.

Damon leaned toward her and lowered his voice. "Just don't keep that boy in Sheridan too long, okay?"

"Believe me, I won't."

"Good." He rapped his knuckles lightly on the counter. "Knew I could count on you to be sensible. He's gone totally around the bend for you. That said, I'm really happy for you guys." Giving her a wink, he turned and followed Phil to a table.

Whitney ducked her head and fought the urge to laugh. Apparently Ty was telegraphing his moves to his family. She wondered if Damon and Phil had been sent here to ask if she'd please send the poor besotted cowboy on his way.

She would, too, but they had an agreement. He'd stay an hour and then leave. She'd hold him to it, but he did deserve something for his patience.

While she continued to work behind the counter filling orders, she occasionally glanced at Damon and Phil's table. They leaned toward each other while they talked and laughed as only a happy couple could do. Watching them gave her heart a lift.

She hadn't expected the invitation to their wedding and she figured it was partly because they liked her. But surely she was being included mostly because of Ty. The wedding was in late June, though, and she wasn't about to predict whether she and Ty would still be seeing each other.

Maybe it didn't matter. Apparently she'd been accepted into the Thunder Mountain crowd, and they didn't strike her as the kind of people who would uninvite her just because she wasn't dating one of their own anymore. They were far classier than that.

Both Damon and Phil waved to her as they left the coffee shop just before seven. She was out the door minutes after. If she knew Ty, he'd already be waiting in the parking lot, watching the clock.

Well, she'd been watching the clock, too. Last night's episode in the back of her car had been memorable, to say the least. This morning she'd put on her red bra and panties as promised and all day they'd been a subtle reminder of Ty.

As she drove, she noticed that decorations had begun appearing in yards and on rooftops. She'd always loved this season when the darkness of winter was chased away as sparkling lights popped up all over town. Sheridan was no different from Cheyenne in that respect.

But this holiday season promised to be even more bright and shiny than usual. She had a new man in her life who was kind, sexy and crazy about her. Christmas and romance were an exhilarating combination, and she relished that extra zing of excitement that Ty contributed.

When she pulled into the parking lot and spotted his truck, anticipation curled in her stomach and sent heat spiraling through her body. By the time she'd climbed out of the car he was there, sweeping her into his arms and claiming her mouth with a kiss that made her forget the icy wind.

She kissed him back with at least as much eagerness. But just as she was beginning to wonder if they'd spend the entire hour making out in the parking lot, he drew back.

Grabbing her hand, he squeezed it. "Let's go in."

"Where's your hat?" She'd been so busy kissing him she hadn't noticed he wasn't wearing it. She didn't want to leave it lying in a snow bank.

"In the truck. Figured it was an unnecessary distraction." He grinned. "If you know what I mean."

"Gotcha." She locked the car and they hurried to the

front door. Once they were inside, he pulled her up the stairs and down the hall, clearly a man on a mission. She didn't need urging. Their goals were aligned.

She unlocked her apartment door and he hustled her through it, kicking it shut with his booted foot. After that, everything was a blur of Christmas lights, the scent of pine and uncontrolled lust. Coats came off somehow, and then they tumbled onto the futon because it was the nearest horizontal surface.

Shoving her skirt to her waist, he wrenched off her panties. She lost one shoe but still wore the other when he opened his fly, rolled on a condom and moved between her thighs. Holding her gaze, he drove into her with enough force to lift her off the futon.

With a startled cry of pure pleasure, she erupted. Her climax must have triggered his because he groaned once before locking himself against her, his body shuddering.

He squeezed his eyes shut, and when he opened them, they glowed with happiness. "Welcome home."

12

TY HAD NEVER taken a woman that quickly. He'd feel a little guilty except for the gleam of wonder and satisfaction in Whitney's brown eyes. Apparently she'd liked it.

She sucked in a ragged breath. "I've never felt so welcomed in my life."

Leaning down, he brushed his mouth against hers. "There's more where that came from." Judging from the tension building in his groin, he'd only taken the edge off. "But here's an idea. Let's move to the bedroom."

Her response was to pull him into a deep kiss with lots of tongue.

He was breathing fast and getting hard again by the time she released him. He chuckled. "Or not. We can stay right here. I have plenty of condoms in my pocket."

Breathing pretty fast herself, she smiled up at him. "Ready for anything?"

"You name it, lady. You never did give me that list."

"You just checked one off."

"Which one?"

"Frantic, still wearing most of our clothes, quickie sex."

"Good guess on my part, huh?"

"Excellent, considering I didn't even know I wanted that." She stroked his cheek. "But now I want naked in a comfy bed sex."

"I could go for some of that myself." He eased away from her. "Tell you what. I'll head for your bathroom and meet you in your bedroom."

"Deal. Give me five minutes, okay?"

"Okay." He wasn't sure what she needed five minutes for, but he'd give her the moon on a silver platter. If she wanted to sacrifice a couple extra minutes of their time together, he'd go along.

He took his time disposing of the condom, tucking in his shirt, zipping his fly and buckling his belt. He'd be reversing the process almost immediately, but walking into a woman's bedroom with his fly open wasn't his idea of smooth.

When he'd stalled long enough, he turned off the bathroom light and walked across the hall to find out what she was up to. In the doorway he stopped and caught his breath. "Wow."

She'd made damn good use of those five minutes. Instead of the bedside lamps, candles glowed on her dresser and bedside tables. Their flickering light revealed Whitney, wearing her red panties and bra, stretched out on snowy-white sheets. She'd taken her hair out of its ponytail and it fell in soft waves around her face and neck.

Best of all was her smile, a combination of mischief and sensuality. She fingered the clasp of her bra and her voice was low and smoky with desire. "Gonna stand there all night, cowboy, or meander on over here and see what I have for you?"

He swallowed and fought the urge to cover the distance in two quick strides. "I'm taking a mental picture."

"Oh." She cupped her breasts and massaged gently. "Still shot or video?"

Primitive urges threatened to turn him into an animal. He struggled to hold that raging beast in check. "Both."

"I wouldn't mind having some mental pictures of my own." She slipped a finger under the lacey edge of her bra and ran it slowly back and forth. "Watching you strip is on my list."

The beast inside him strained at its tether. "All right." He started on the snaps of his shirt. "But you've seen this part."

"Not when you were standing right in front of me." She slid her hand free and ran her finger along the top edge of her panties. "Not when I could watch your chest heave like that."

Dear God, she was driving him insane. He followed the progress of her teasing finger as he tossed his shirt to the floor. Then he propped his hips against the dresser while he pulled off his boots and socks.

All the while she stroked her finger along the elastic holding those panties snug around her hips. If she'd put them back on to make him crazy, she'd succeeded. He was cross-eyed with the lust pumping through his veins.

As he unbuckled his belt and unfastened the top button of his jeans, she began fingering the elastic at the top of her thigh. He groaned. "Whitney…"

"What?" Her eyes widened in mock innocence. Then she deliberately slid her finger under the elastic and touched herself. "Is something bothering you?"

"Only the fit of my jeans." And he shucked them, along with his briefs. He was rewarded by her sharp intake of breath. "You were saying?" He walked toward the bed.

Her eyes darkened. "The…the condoms are back in the drawer…again."

"Good to know." He climbed into bed and gently guided her onto her back. "For later."

She gazed up at him. "Later?"

"Yes, ma'am." Sliding down her sleek body, he slowly began peeling off those red panties. "I don't know if this is on your list, but it's on mine."

"I…" She shivered beneath him. "That would be…" She sucked in another breath. "Nice."

"I thought so." His heart hammered as he uncovered the soft blond triangle he'd been unable to see the night before. The rich aroma of desire filled his nostrils, making him dizzy with wanting her. His voice roughened with anticipation. "Very nice." He blew on her damp curls.

"Ty…" The slight note of pleading and the restless shift of her hips gave her away. She wanted this, too.

He slipped her panties over her smooth thighs and down past her shapely calves. Once they were gone, he began a leisurely trip back, kissing and nibbling his way to her sweet center. He'd missed being able to see her the night before. Now candlelight flickered over her fair skin and he was relishing every second.

She began to tremble and her breathing grew quick and shallow. "*Ty.*"

"Mmm?" He glanced up.

Propped on her elbows, her cheeks flushed, she watched him. "You're…" She cleared her throat. "You're torturing me."

"You don't like it?"

She flopped back on the bed. "No, I don't like it, I *love* it. But then I think about the time."

"Don't worry about the time." He went back to the

erotic pleasure of running his tongue over her satin thighs.

"One of us has to!"

"Then let that person be me." He nudged her legs a little farther apart. Ah. Perfect.

"But—"

"Shhh." He placed a lingering kiss inches from his ultimate destination. "Let me love you."

She groaned. "Okay! Just don't forget you have to leave."

"I won't. I promise." And he bestowed the most intimate kiss of all. She surrendered with such joyful abandon that he instantly regretted that promise.

Oh, this was going to be good. He savored the taste of passion on his tongue as he explored her slick heat. When she began to moan and thrash, he slid both hands under her hips. Holding her fast, he went deeper. Her body bowed and clenched until...*yes*. Amid the music of her wild cries, he drank the ambrosia of her climax.

The perfection of that moment helped him ignore the persistent throbbing of his cock and the painful tightening of his balls. But as her tremors subsided, he couldn't ignore the ache any longer. He'd take her once more, just once, and then he'd go.

He moved away slowly with soft kisses and light caresses and climbed out of bed.

She struggled for breath. "Are you leaving?"

"Not yet." He opened the bedside table drawer and took out one of the loose condoms. In the flickering light from the candles he glanced at the little clock sitting there. There was still time to do this right.

Tearing open the packet, he rolled on the condom.

"You're beautiful."

He glanced toward the bed. She'd settled on her side

and her gaze was fastened on his package. Sliding back in beside her, he cupped her face and looked into her eyes. "No, you're beautiful. I'm just functional."

She smiled. "Are you planning to demonstrate that functionality any time soon?"

"I thought I would, but first, let's undo this. I didn't get around to that before." He reached for the clasp of her bra and flicked it open.

"I enjoyed what you did get around to."

"I hope so." Looking into her eyes, he pushed her bra aside and stroked her warm breast. "I'm hoping you enjoy the next part, too."

"I already am." Her voice was a soft purr of contentment. "You're very good with your hands, Mr. Slater."

He cupped her fullness and squeezed gently as he brushed his thumb over her nipple. "I could touch you like this for hours."

"This weekend."

"Count on it." He urged her to her back and moved over her. "I'll be here." Holding her gaze, he sought her entrance with his cock and slid effortlessly into her welcoming heat. "Right here." *Home.* He hadn't imagined the feeling last night. Nothing had ever felt so perfect.

Grasping his hips, she lifted up, cinching them in tighter. "I'll be thinking about that all week."

"Good." He eased back and pushed home again as he watched her eyes darken. "Think about how it feels when I bury myself deep inside you like this." He drew away and thrust forward. "And this." Pumping slowly, he leaned down and grazed her lips with his. "Think about how you quiver and tighten around my cock."

She moaned and held on as he increased the pace.

"Think about how my tongue feels when my head is between your thighs." He lowered his mouth to hers and mimicked the steady movement of his hips with his tongue. He felt the quickening deep inside, the first twitch of her orgasm.

His climax hovered near, but he clamped down on the impulse. He could wait. Oh, yes, he could wait, knowing that she was almost there. He lifted his head and pumped faster. "Come for me."

"Yes…" She gasped.

"That's it. Let go."

"Oh, Ty… *Ty.*"

He gritted his teeth as the waves of her orgasm rolled over his rigid cock. He wouldn't come, not yet. He knew what he wanted, thought they could achieve it. Gradually her spasms eased. Drawing back, he pushed in again.

Her body vibrated in reaction. Good sign.

"You're going to come again," he murmured, gazing down at her.

She sucked in a breath and nodded.

"I'll be with you this time." Watching her eyes, he began to thrust with more force. Right on cue she shuddered and began to tighten and pulse in that lovely way that told him she was heading for another climax.

He responded with firm, steady strokes, building the tension as color bloomed in her cheeks and her eyes darkened. Her breasts quivered as she gasped for breath. And then he felt something change, as if she'd opened to him and he could touch her very core.

The blood sang in his veins. This, *this* was the ultimate connection. He drove in over and over, glorying in each moment he returned to that haven.

She trembled, poised on the edge, so close…*there*. She cried out. With a roar of triumph he plunged into her again and they both came, swirling in the wild release together, clinging to each other and gasping for breath.

Her face became a blur as his eyes lost focus. Then gradually, as he stopped shaking, his gaze found hers. She looked as dazzled as he felt. For a while they just stared at each other.

Finally she took a ragged breath. "Okay, I'll go first. Are you an alien from outer space?"

He laughed. Whatever he'd expected her to say, it hadn't been that. "Why do you ask?"

"See?" She smiled. "You must be or you would have denied it right away."

"I'm not an alien from outer space. I'm a lawyer from Cheyenne."

"Sorry, but I don't believe you. The sex just keeps getting better and it was amazing to start with. I may not be the most experienced girl, but I've had a couple of decently equipped boyfriends with good skills. You just blew them right out of the water."

"Yeah?" He couldn't help grinning. "That's great to hear."

"Well, I think you're an alien. That's the only thing that explains all these incredible orgasms. Feels as if you've burrowed deep into my psyche. Like we have some cosmic connection when you're inside me, especially this last time when we came at the same time."

He took a deep breath. "I feel that way, too. And it doesn't make any sense. It's not like we've known each other for years, or even for months. We saw each other a couple of times a week at the coffee shop."

"So what's going on?"

"I don't know." He leaned down and gave her a soft kiss. "I guess we can think about it for the next few days. Right now I have to go. I promised."

She glanced over at the clock. "Yikes. Yes, you do. At

least it'll be clear tonight. I checked the weather report. No more snow for at least a few days."

"I checked it, too." He left the sweet warmth of her body. "Next storm's due around Friday."

"Maybe it won't hit then, or at least not until after you get here."

"That's my hope." He left her bedroom with its romantic candles and cozy bed fragrant with sex. Much as he didn't want to leave, maybe he needed some time alone to think this through. He was getting in deep, and damned fast, too.

After disposing of the condom, he went back to grab his clothes. She'd put on a robe and was picking up his stuff from the floor where he'd dropped it.

"Here, I can do that." He scooped his jeans up along with his briefs.

"I don't want you to be any later than you already are."

He placed a hand on her shoulder. "Whitney, I wanted to be with you tonight. I'd even go so far as to say I was frantic to be with you tonight." As he said it, he felt a little uneasy because it was true.

She gazed up at him. "That bothers you, doesn't it?"

"Um…"

"It does, I can tell. I'm a little freaked out by how well we mesh, too. I can't believe I'm saying this, but what if we take a rain check on this weekend and plan on the weekend after that? That'll give us both a chance to get our bearings."

It was a sensible idea but he had trouble being sensible when they were both naked. "Let me get dressed. I think better when I'm dressed."

"We probably both do." Stepping back, she folded her arms. "That's why this is a good idea. You tried to put the brakes on in the beginning, remember? You wanted us to get acquainted before we got horizontal."

"Which we did, sort of." He pulled on his briefs and then his jeans.

"Maybe if we'd ended up spending the night in my apartment like we planned, we wouldn't have fallen into this scarcity mode where we're scrambling to be alone."

He located his shirt and shoved his arms into the sleeves. "All the more reason to spend a whole weekend together and get over that."

"I'm not so sure. We set it up so that we're hiding out from everybody. That makes it like a lost weekend, as if we have to spend every available minute in bed."

He chuckled as he tucked his shirt into his jeans. "That's pretty much how I envisioned it."

"But it's sort of clandestine, as if what we're doing is forbidden, and you know what they say about forbidden fruit."

"I think I've heard that a time or two." Leaning against the dresser, he pulled on his socks and his boots.

"Then here's what I think would be better. We skip next weekend to have some breathing room. Then the following weekend you drive up but let Rosie and Herb know. You stay at the ranch the first night and I drive out for dinner. Then maybe the second night you come to my place, but we don't make it a secret. I don't think you'd really be comfortable coming to town without telling Rosie and Herb."

"Maybe not." He snapped the cuffs on his shirt. "But just know that Rosie's a true romantic and wants her boys paired up"

"All the more reason for us to slow down. If I read her right, if she found out we'd secretly spent the weekend together, she'd be planning the wedding."

Ty gazed at her and sighed. "I can't deny it. And she would find out. She's like a bloodhound that way. Good luck ever keeping a secret from Rosie."

"Neither one of us is ready for that kind of matchmaking pressure."

"No."

"So it's settled, then? You'll plan a trip to Sheridan in two weeks and we'll get together then? That will telegraph to Rosie—and ourselves—that we're easing into this relationship instead of leaping into it."

He looked at her standing there in her fluffy red robe, her hair tousled from making love, her lips rosy from kissing and her eyes sparkling from all those orgasms. What she'd said was absolutely the right course of action but… "I want to be with you next weekend. I want to hold you, and kiss you, and—"

"I know." She swallowed. "I want you, too. But if we really do have something special going on, we should allow it to develop slowly over time. Red-hot affairs burn out. At least that's what I've heard."

"Okay." He rubbed the back of his neck and wondered if he'd unconsciously counted on having a red-hot affair that burned out quickly. It would be less likely to detonate any land mines than a prolonged relationship. "I'd love to see you next weekend, but okay."

"The time will go fast."

With a groan he eliminated the space between them and pulled her into his arms. "It'll go agonizingly slow and you know it." Capturing her mouth, he vented every ounce of his frustration in the heat of his goodbye kiss. And because he knew she was naked under the robe, he loosened the tie and stroked her breast until she pushed him away, gasping for air.

"Get out of here, cowboy, before I drag you back to bed."

If he hadn't promised, he would have let her do it. But he was a man of his word. "See you in two weeks."

He made it outside in record time and when the cold hit his overheated body he groaned. Maybe he'd needed that blast of icy air the same way people needed a hard slap. Time to face reality.

On the drive back to Cheyenne he admitted that when it came to Whitney, he was confused. He didn't know whether to jump in with both feet and hope for the best or run like hell from emotions that kept him off-balance. This cooling-off period that he'd fought against might be exactly what he needed.

Naive as it might have been, he'd always imagined that someday he'd meet a woman who was perfect for him and they'd live happily ever after. That someday was now and Whitney was the one. He'd probably known that the first time she'd filled his coffee order. He should be ecstatic that he'd found—as Rosie would put it—the love of his life.

And on one level he was. Their shared pleasure was effortless and magical. She obviously loved being naked with him and he loved being naked with her…physically. But he had a bad feeling that eventually she'd expect him to be naked emotionally, too. And that terrified him.

He simply wasn't capable of that kind of soul-baring intimacy, not even for someone as terrific as Whitney. Maybe if the sex was good enough and their time together was filled with laughter and easy companionship, she wouldn't ask to see into the dark recesses of his psyche. That wasn't a particularly solid plan, but the alternative was giving her up and he couldn't do it.

13

TY HAD BEEN absolutely right. The two weeks away from each other were endless. Whitney couldn't say she'd had much insight into their situation during that time, either. But she did find it interesting that at first he'd wanted to slow down and then she had.

Maybe they both realized this wasn't an ordinary love affair. Their passion for each other was explosive, not to mention the underlying deep connection they both felt when they were locked together. That kind of emotional power should be handled with care so they didn't blow each other to smithereens.

Still, she missed him terribly. When she thought of his kiss, his touch and his beautiful body—and she thought of all those things on a regular basis—she ached for him.

Because she was resourceful when it came to beating the blues, she filled her spare time buying Christmas presents for her family, including something for the Secret Santa exchange they did every year. Then she contacted Phil to set up a time to tour Thunder Mountain Academy.

They played phone tag and didn't find a time to get together until Thursday afternoon, the day before Ty was scheduled to drive back up from Cheyenne. That was just as well. She and Ty had managed a few phone conversations, but they always seemed to deteriorate into suggestive comments that created even more frustration.

When she had a little more than twenty-four hours before his ETA, any distraction was welcome. She met Phil at the ranch house, and Rosie joined them. As they walked from the house to the meadow where the cabins were located, Whitney glanced up at the sky and the gray clouds moving in.

"Don't worry," Rosie said. "This'll blow through. I checked the weather this morning. Ty will make it up here, no problem."

"I'm sure he will." Whitney didn't believe in buying trouble, but she'd lived in Wyoming all her life. Those looked like snow clouds. She'd been watching the forecast all week and what Rosie had said was correct according to the weather gurus. She hoped they were right because she was desperate to see that cowboy.

They toured the rec room first, the most recent addition to the meadow. The heat was turned way down in all the buildings to conserve energy so they all left their coats on.

"Damon should really be here for this part because the rec room is his baby," Phil said. "But he made a quick run to Billings today. A guy's selling a barely used table saw and Damon thinks we need a replacement for the one we have. The guy does love his tools."

Whitney glanced around the mostly empty room. "This place is huge!"

"It seems that way now," Rosie said, "but wait until we get a bunch of teenagers in it. We've ordered a second pool table that should arrive any time, plus tables and chairs for meals, but it'll also double as a classroom."

"I can't wait," Phil said. "I just know they're going to love being at the ranch."

"I'll bet they will." Whitney had no trouble imagining it. "A small group of kids around the same age, all focused on a subject they're really interested in—what could be better for learning? It's like Hogwarts for horse lovers."

Phil laughed. "That's a perfect description. I'll remember that when I'm talking to people about it. No magic spells or incantations, but if you're a kid who loves horses, this place will be magical."

"It will." Whitney gazed around the empty room and pictured it with classes in progress. "I have a cousin who would eat this up with a spoon. I'm not sure my aunt and uncle can afford it, though."

"We're looking into getting sponsors to donate scholarships," Rosie said. "Boot and hat companies are on our list. We've had interest from feed companies, too. Ben Radcliffe's doing so well with his saddle business he's thinking of offering one scholarship per semester. Is your cousin a good student?"

"Oh, yeah, Dee Ann's amazing. Honor student, into all kinds of school activities, loves horses. I'll mention it privately to my aunt and uncle and let them know scholarships might be a possibility. A semester here would be an incredible opportunity for her."

"She sounds like exactly the kind of young woman we want to enroll in the program," Phil said. "Come on. Let's go see the cabins. Then you'll get even more excited."

Phil's enthusiasm was catching. Instead of simply looking around one of the cabins, Whitney climbed into a loft bed to check out the room from that angle.

"Good idea. I've wanted to do that ever since they were built." Rosie took the one across from Whitney.

"They really are fun." Phil claimed the bed next to Rosie's and sat there swinging her feet. "I don't think you ever outgrow your love of the top bunk."

Whitney flopped onto the bare mattress. "Takes me back to my slumber party days, only the setting wasn't as awesome as this. My sister and I—" She caught herself. She hadn't meant to mention Selena to anyone in Sheridan, but maybe it was time to start. This might be as good a place as any.

"I didn't realize you have a sister," Phil said. "Does she live in Cheyenne?"

Propping herself up on her elbow, Whitney looked over at Phil. She wanted to be able to assure her new friend that the question and the necessary answer wouldn't cause a problem. "Selena died in a car accident when we were sixteen. We were twins."

"Oh!" Phil's eyes widened and she flushed. "Whitney, I didn't—"

"It's okay." She sat up. "Nobody in Sheridan knows, but it's not a touchy subject at all."

"Oh, honey." Rosie gazed at her. "That must have been so tough, though."

"Maybe it's still tough," Phil said. "I'm really sorry, Whitney. Your twin sister. Yikes."

"It's not as bad as it could be. My folks did the right thing and got us all counseling. When I'm with my family in Cheyenne, Selena's not a forbidden subject. We reminisce about the good times. It's a huge help."

Rosie nodded. "That would be very healing. When I worked in social services, we encouraged people to do that."

"It's great, and I'm in pretty good shape emotionally.

But I haven't said anything since I moved here because I want people to get to know me first. I don't want it to be my defining characteristic. In Cheyenne, everyone who was around back then remembers but it's faded in everyone's mind, so it's not the first thing they think of when they see me."

"I so get that," Phil said. "Just like when I moved here I didn't go around telling everyone that my mom died when I was a little kid. It's part of who I am, but not the most important part."

Whitney smiled at her. "Exactly."

"So I'm guessing Ty doesn't know this, either," Rosie said.

"I haven't told him yet. It's not the sort of thing you bring up right away in a new relationship."

"Of course not," Phil said. "That reference to your sister probably slipped out by accident because we were reliving our slumber party days."

"Yep. Although maybe it's a good thing. Maybe I've been in town long enough that I can tell a few people."

"But we won't," Rosie said. "Who you tell and when is your choice to make."

"I appreciate that. And I don't mind at all that you both know. But with Ty, it's more complicated. I could be wrong, but I get the sense he hasn't completely dealt with what happened to him."

"He hasn't." Rosie sighed. "It's difficult because he doesn't have anybody to mourn with or reminisce with. His parents were older when they had him so the grandparents were gone on both sides. He has one uncle who dealt with his brother's death by climbing into a bottle so he's no help."

"See, that's another reason I have to tread lightly. Judging from what you're saying, the way my parents and I have handled Selena's death wouldn't work for him. In fact, hearing about it might actually make him feel worse because he can't go that route."

"Are you sure he couldn't?" Phil hopped down from the bunk. "His parents must have had close friends. What about them? They could reminisce with him, couldn't they?"

Rosie shook her head. "The couple closest to them had hoped to adopt Ty. He turned into such a holy terror that they gave up and brought him to us. He was making their family miserable."

"Wow." Whitney couldn't picture Ty as a holy terror.

"To his credit, he tried to find them a few years ago so he could make amends, but they'd moved and their last name is Brown, so they'd be hard to trace."

"Like Jones," Whitney said. "That's why I have an unusual first name. Anyway, props to you and Herb for taking him in and calming him down."

"Herb and I can't claim all the credit. Listening to the other guys' horror stories did the most good. Putting all those boys together was like tossing them in a rock tumbler. The rough edges came off."

Phil nodded. "You can see that when they interact. They still tumble against each other sometimes. I thought Damon and Cade were going to come to blows at the Fourth of July party, but then they just went off and drank beer together."

"Typical." Rosie smiled. "Ty and Brant are like that with each other. I don't know that Ty would have come around without Brant Ellison."

"He's mentioned Brant," Whitney said. "I was hoping to meet him but I'll be in Cheyenne when he's here for Christmas."

"You'll meet everyone for sure at the wedding," Phil

said. "Right, Rosie? We're inviting the world to this ceremony."

"Everyone in Damon's world, that's for sure. I'm counting on you to add the names of everyone in your world. That's the beauty of having it at the ranch. We don't have to limit the guest list."

"And I'm thrilled to be included considering I'm so new in town," Whitney said.

Phil glanced up at her. "Funny, but you don't feel new. It seems as if I've known you longer than five months."

"Same here." Rosie gave Whitney a fond glance. "You've made a big impression already. Everybody I know loves Rangeland Roasters."

Whitney laughed. "Because everybody loves you and you talk me up."

"*No.*" Rosie's cheeks turned pink. "It's because you're nice and you serve great coffee in a cheerful shop."

"Which she tells people all the time," Phil said. "So you're right, she's your best advertisement, but she wouldn't do it unless she believed in you."

"Aw." Whitney's throat felt tight. "Thank you both."

"You're welcome." Rosie smiled at her. "And on that lovely note, I suggest we head back to the house and warm up with a cup of coffee. It won't be as fancy as yours, Whitney, but I can offer you a touch of Baileys."

WHITNEY ACCEPTED THE coffee and Baileys although Phil had told her privately she didn't have to drink it if that wasn't her thing. But Whitney liked it well enough, and Rosie seemed happy to serve it to her.

She ended up staying for dinner, and by the time she left around eight, big flakes of snow were falling. She switched on the radio and the forecast hadn't changed—a few flurries tonight and tomorrow but mostly clear. She wished she believed it.

The snowflakes grew thicker and more numerous as she drove. By the time she'd parked and made it into her apartment, it was officially snowing hard, no matter what the weather folks claimed on TV. She wasn't surprised when Ty called her cell.

"Don't worry. This'll clear up," he said in a confident tone.

"I'm sure it will." She refused to be Debby Downer when he seemed so positive. "I toured the rec hall and the cabins today."

"Yeah? Pretty cool, huh?"

"It'll be a fabulous experience for the kids. Rosie said there might be scholarships, so I'm hoping my cousin Dee Ann can go."

"That'd be great. How many cousins did you say you have?"

"Fourteen. Six on my dad's side and eight on my mom's side."

"Fertile family."

"Thus the plethora of condoms I keep on hand."

He laughed. "Okay, let the record show that tonight it's your fault that the conversation veered toward sex."

"You brought up fertility."

"You could have let that comment go, but instead you linked it to the condoms in your bedside table drawer."

"You're right, counselor." She smiled. "I miss you so much. I hope this snow doesn't—"

"It won't. Even if it does, the heat I'm feeling right now will melt whatever stands in my way. I'm coming for you, lady."

Moisture sluiced between her thighs. "I suspect I'll be coming for you, too, cowboy."

"I guaran-damn-tee you will if I have anything to say about it. Which I plan to."

"You realize we're *this* close to having phone sex."

"I'm holding out for the real thing, myself."

"Me, too, but you're supposed to stay at the ranch tomorrow night after dinner as I recall, while I drive home to my lonely apartment."

He groaned. "Who dreamed up that stupid idea?"

"Me, because then you aren't sneaking into town, and I'm totally on board with the plan."

"Party pooper."

"I really am in favor of you spending the night there, Ty. Rosie's looking forward to it and she deserves to have time with you. We'll have Saturday night to ourselves."

"What color underwear are you wearing Saturday night?"

"What color do you want?"

"Black."

"You've got it."

"What color do you have on now?"

"I'm not going there, cowboy. We really are in the phone sex danger zone. See you tomorrow night at the ranch!" And she disconnected.

He texted her immediately. I'm guessing pale blue.

Wrong. Good night, Ty.

Purple?

Nope. Sweet dreams.

I'd tell you what I'll be dreaming except it'll melt the phone.

Good night, Ty. She switched off her phone because if she didn't, they would keep this up until they were both frustrated as hell. Walking to the window, she cupped her hands around her face so she could see outside. Damn, it was snowing even harder.

Her alarm went off before dawn the next morning, and when she turned on her TV, the weather report finally admitted they were in for a blizzard. She left messages for all her employees to stay home. Then she threw on some clothes, drove to the shop amid buffeting winds and put a sign on the inside of the door.

Surely no one would come looking for coffee in this weather, but if they did, they'd learn that the shop would be open when the blizzard had passed, whenever that happened to be. The way the wind was howling, she didn't expect it to be anytime soon. She didn't expect Ty to drive up from Cheyenne, either, and disappointment curdled in her stomach.

Once she was back home, she texted him. Don't try it.

His reply was instantaneous. I won't until it's safe.

Her shoulders sagged with relief. No matter how much she longed to have him here, she didn't want him taking foolish chances. Thank goodness he wasn't the type who would.

The blizzard raged all day and into the night. She exchanged texts with Rosie, who had resigned herself to a change of plans. So had Whitney. Even if the storm petered out, having Ty drive up for one night was insane. She played Christmas carols and wrapped packages, something she'd need to do anyway before she drove to Cheyenne on Christmas Eve in a couple of weeks.

When the weather didn't improve at all on Saturday, she felt fortunate to have food in the apartment and power to her appliances. Mother Nature had shut down all activity with a breathtaking show of power. So she wrote Christmas cards, a job she'd been putting off for days.

She hadn't heard from Ty, which meant either he was having trouble getting cell phone service or he was royally pissed that they wouldn't see each other this weekend. She was willing to believe either or both possibilities. Her one text to him—There's always next weekend!—wasn't answered.

Saturday night, when she should have been rolling around in bed with Ty, she watched a movie on TV that didn't hold her interest. Eventually she climbed under the covers and turned out the light. Her usual optimistic outlook was a little tarnished because she really missed Ty. Too bad they hadn't started this affair in the summer.

A persistent buzzing noise woke her up. At first she panicked, thinking it was the fire alarm because she'd left something on the stove without realizing it. No, it wasn't the fire alarm. It was her intercom. She glanced at her bedside clock. Two in the morning.

It had to be Ty. No one else would show up at two without calling. And she was wearing her flannel nightgown with rosebuds on it. Racing to the living room, she flipped the switch. "Ty?"

He sounded exhausted. "It's me. I need you."

Heart pounding, she activated the front door lock. Then she ran barefoot into the hall. She'd started down the stairs when he met her halfway, his face haggard and his coat and hat dusted with snow. He clutched a duffel bag in his right hand.

Diving into his arms, she hugged him and felt him stagger. She hugged him tighter and absorbed the chill of his sheepskin coat. "You idiot! What the hell were you thinking?"

"That I had to see you." His arms came around her and the duffel bumped her hip. They stayed like that, holding each other, until he finally sighed and loosened his grip. "It's okay, now. I made it. Let's go upstairs."

They walked up the steps in tandem, their arms around each other. "You're crazy," she said. "I hope you know that."

"No, I'm not. I followed a snowplow. You can't go off the road when you follow a snowplow."

"I should be really mad at you for this stunt."

"But you're not. I can tell because you ran out to meet me. Sexy nightgown, by the way." Even when he was exhausted, he apparently couldn't resist teasing her.

"It's the granny gown I wear when I'm not expecting anyone, and I certainly wasn't expecting *you*, cowboy." She wanted to lecture him about being stupid, but she couldn't. He'd gone through hell and a blizzard to be with her, and that was heroic, in a dumb sort of way.

He wasn't moving very fast, and he leaned against her as they walked. She glanced up at him. "How long have you been on the road?"

"Not sure. I think I started out around three this afternoon."

"Three? But that's almost twelve hours!"

His chuckle was ragged. "Time flies when you're having fun."

She maneuvered him through her open apartment door. He was still holding on to her as if without her support he might collapse. Leaving the door open for now, she walked him into the bedroom and over to the bed. "Lie down."

"Okay." He dropped the duffel and collapsed onto the bed, clothes, boots and all. Somewhere along the way he'd lost his hat. He gazed up at her, his gray eyes dull with fatigue. "Are you getting in with me?"

"In a minute." She hurried back to the living room so she could lock up. Then she scooped up his hat from where it had fallen on the floor. By the time she returned, he was asleep.

Although he was deadweight, she managed to work him out of his boots and socks plus both sleeves of his coat. Pulling the coat out from under him proved to be impossible. Sleeping with a belt on wouldn't feel very good, so she unbuckled it, but she couldn't tug it loose, either.

In his place, she'd want her jeans unbuttoned, too. How strange to be performing that intimate task when he was asleep instead of aroused and desperate to have her. He looked so vulnerable lying there.

Then again, she'd never seen him sleeping. Every time they'd been together he'd been awake, loaded with testosterone and ready to make love. This quiet moment allowed her a glimpse of the young boy who'd had both parents yanked from his life in an instant. With no siblings, no close relatives to cling to, he'd lost everything.

Judging from Rosie's description, he'd responded with anger. He'd gotten past that with the help of Rosie, Herb and his foster brothers. On the surface, at least, he seemed at peace, as he'd proudly announced to her.

But he was a man who needed a deep emotional connection, whether he could admit it or not. She might never have known that if they hadn't made love. She'd seen wonder in his eyes, the same wonder she'd felt, but she'd also seen fear. A man with his past could be terrified that making that connection meant risking the loss of it. She couldn't blame him.

If he wanted to believe their relationship was mostly

sexual, she'd go along for now. But she didn't know how he could keep fooling himself when he'd driven twelve hours through a blizzard to see her. Once he realized she was becoming critical to his happiness, he might run like the wind. Then they'd both lose.

14

TY WOKE WITH a start and stared into the darkness. Was he still driving? Had he fallen asleep at the wheel and run into a snowbank? No, he was in a bed. Whitney's bed. Gradually he remembered getting to her apartment complex and stumbling up the stairs with her. God, how pathetic.

She'd been wearing a granny gown and he'd joked about it. But he hadn't made love to her. He would have remembered that. In any case, she must have led him in here although he couldn't recall the exact sequence of events.

He could hear her slow, even breathing next to him. Turning his head, he saw her lying on her side facing him, but her eyes were closed and she'd pulled the covers up to her chin. He, on the other hand, was on top of the covers. Apparently she'd put a blanket over him so he wouldn't get cold. Once he'd conked out, he must have been too heavy for her to move.

He pictured himself collapsing, fully dressed, onto her bed. Lovely. And wearing his boots, too? He hoped to hell not. Wiggling his toes, he ascertained that he wasn't wearing socks, let alone boots, but he might have been when he'd flopped down on her green comforter.

Bad form, Slater. Bad form. Moving carefully so he wouldn't wake her, he eased out from under the blanket. He'd swallowed gallons of coffee on the way up here and he needed to make a quick trip across the hall. When he stood, his belt jangled and he realized it was unbuckled. The button on his jeans was undone, too. He doubted she'd done that in hopes of some action. Probably she'd tried to make him as comfortable as possible considering he'd been unconscious and impossible to budge.

Holding his belt so it wouldn't rattle, he managed one step before he tripped over something soft and went down with a thud. Damn. He'd likely woken her and anyone sleeping in the room below. He was one smooth operator this weekend.

"Ty?" She switched on a lamp. "Are you okay?"

"Fine." He got to his feet and turned back to her. "Sorry. Tripped over my duffel." A glance at the bedside clock told him it was a little past four. He'd sailed in at two, interrupted her sleep, and now, two hours later, he'd interrupted it again.

She sat up, rubbed her eyes and yawned, exactly like a little girl might. "I should have moved it. Forgot."

"I should have remembered it was there." He was transfixed by the sight of her in that granny gown. The combination of the sweet little rosebuds and no makeup made her look about ten years old. Then she straightened her shoulders and her breasts moved under the flannel. Nope, not ten. His cock twitched.

"Can I get you something?"

"No, I just…" He gestured toward the bathroom.

"Sure, sure." She made shooing motions with her hand. "That was a long drive."

"Yeah, it was." An insanely long drive. He probably needed to look long and hard at his reasons for making it. But for now, he had something more basic to take care of. He walked into the bathroom, closed the door and turned on the light. Then he caught a glimpse of some raggedy stranger in the mirror.

The stranger turned out to be him, and damn, he couldn't remember the last time he'd looked this bad. Scruffy beard, hair sticking out every which way, bloodshot eyes. Shitfire. Whitney must be dying to get a piece of this.

After taking care of his most urgent problem, he fastened his jeans but took his belt off. He'd get it later.

Returning to the sink, he washed his hands and splashed cold water on his face. It didn't improve his reflection any, but his eyes felt a little less gritty. While his hands were still wet he finger-combed his hair into something more presentable.

He couldn't do anything about the bristles unless he fetched his shaving kit out of his duffel. Settling back down so they could both get some sleep was a higher priority. He turned off the light and walked back into the bedroom.

She was still sitting up with the light on as if she'd been waiting for him. "You probably didn't have a decent dinner. If you're hungry, I can fix you something. It won't be fancy, but I have some eggs and bread for toast. I even have homemade jam from my mom."

Sounded heavenly. He hadn't eaten since grabbing a quick lunch before leaving. But he wasn't about to have her get up and make him something. "That's okay. Let's just go back to sleep." His stomach rumbled loud enough that he knew she'd heard it.

She laughed and threw back the covers. "Come on. Neither of us will get any sleep with that going on."

"You can go back to bed. I'll have a slice of bread and jam and that'll take care of me."

She shook her head as she shoved her feet into a pair of fuzzy pink slippers. "I'm awake, now, and I doubt I'll go back to sleep while you're rattling around in my kitchen. Unless the blizzard's let up and the roads are all cleared, I won't be opening Rangeland Roasters this morning, so no worries."

He followed her into the kitchen, watching her hips move under the soft flannel. She wouldn't be wearing anything under that nightgown. "I kept the radio on while I drove, and they said to expect heavy snow until late this afternoon. Nobody will be on the road today except emergency vehicles and snowplows."

She sighed. "Oh, well. Good thing business has been great until now. Our bottom line won't be hit too hard, but I worry about my employees. I pay them by the hour and when they don't work for several days, it has to hurt."

"I hadn't considered that." Selfish jerk that he was, he'd only thought about the joy of snuggling with her all morning because she wouldn't be going in to work.

"I'll find a way to make it up to them." She opened the refrigerator and took out a carton of eggs. "Next week I'll spend less time behind the counter and give them extra shifts. I'll find out if anybody has a rent or car payment due and they can have first pick of hours."

"You're a good boss."

"Thanks." She smiled at him. "That's my goal."

"What can I do to help?" He leaned against the counter as she bustled around grabbing a frying pan and a bowl from a cupboard and butter from the refrigerator.

"Make toast." She took a toaster from a bottom cupboard and plugged it in. Then she put a loaf of cinnamon bread on the counter and a jar of cherry jam.

"I'd be happy to." He hated to admit it, but he was starving now that food was being offered. Watching her move around the kitchen was giving him a sexual appetite, too, but after barging in here without warning, he'd settle for a meal. He'd seen himself in the bathroom mirror. He wouldn't blame her if she'd rather feed him eggs and toast than have sex with him.

While butter melted in the pan, she beat the eggs with a wire whisk. The motion made her breasts jiggle, and yes, he noticed that, too. She poured the mixture into the pan and the sizzle fit his mood. If he had his way, they'd eat this in bed and satisfy both his hungers, but he wasn't going to suggest it.

She used a wooden spoon to stir the eggs as they began to cook. After she added some salt and pepper, she glanced over her shoulder. "What do you want to drink?"

"Not coffee. I've had enough to last me a lifetime. Whoops, that might sound offensive to a barista." He spread jam on two slices of warm toast and then popped two more pieces of bread into the toaster.

"I'm not offended. How about cocoa?"

"I could go for that."

"Me, too. I even have a can of whipped cream. Unless you're a marshmallow guy."

"Nope. Always liked whipped cream better."

"All righty, then." She turned off the heat under the frying pan. "Those will be fine for a couple of minutes while I make some cocoa."

He'd never felt so domestic in his life. He wanted cocoa and he wanted her. Upon arriving he'd joked about the flannel nightgown, but it was growing sexier by the minute. Knowing her naked, luscious body was concealed under all those rosebuds fired his imagination. The combination of wholesome and erotic was damn near irresistible.

At least one of his appetites needed to be satisfied ASAP. "Do you mind if I eat some of this toast? I'm hungrier than I thought."

"Please do. I have another loaf in the freezer. Cinnamon bread, peanut butter and cherry jam are what I stock in for blizzard conditions."

"You have peanut butter?"

"I do." She grabbed another pan from the cupboard and began measuring out sugar and cocoa. "In the refrigerator. Help yourself."

He rummaged around and found the jar—creamy, just the way he liked it. He knew from listening to his married friends in Cheyenne that a relationship could rise and fall over crunchy versus smooth. He and Whitney wouldn't have that argument or the other one about marshmallows versus whipped cream.

Then he paused, a table knife resting in the gooey peanut butter. It wasn't all that surprising that he'd think of marriage after driving twelve hours through a blizzard to be with her. People didn't generally do that kind of thing unless they were extremely attached to someone.

Being extremely attached often led to marriage and most aspects of that scenario appealed to him—just not the part where his dearly beloved asked him to haul the picture albums out of the closet. But who knew? Maybe she wouldn't ask. Maybe he'd never have to do that.

He spread peanut butter on top of the jam. That was a back-assed way to do it, but he was too hungry to care. After eating the first piece of toast in three bites, he polished off the second one about the time the toaster popped again. He doctored those up real quick and ate them, too. Then he turned to find her watching him.

He gave her a sheepish smile. "Guess I was hungry."

"Guess so." She turned off the heat under the steaming cocoa and came toward him. "You have jam on your cheek." She reached up and swiped at it with the tip of her finger.

He caught her hand. "Can't be wasting it. That's excellent jam." He sucked it off her finger. He'd meant it as a playful gesture, but the second her finger was in his mouth, everything changed.

Before he could stop himself, he'd pulled her close. He gave one brief thought to his beard, but he had zero control. He kissed her as if his life depended on it.

She kissed him back with such energy that he figured neither of them was in the mood for subtlety. Gathering up the warm flannel of the nightgown, he bunched it at her waist so he could reach between her thighs, her very *damp* thighs. That electric discovery disconnected his brain entirely.

When he swept her up in his arms, her slippers fell to the floor. No matter. She wouldn't need slippers for what he had in mind. Carrying her back to the bedroom, he tumbled with her onto the bed.

Lust raged through him as he yanked open the bedside table drawer and grabbed a condom. He likely set a record for opening his jeans and rolling one on. She was breathing as hard as he was as she lifted her nightgown and opened her thighs.

With a groan of pure joy, he sank into the warm, receptive haven of her body. Locked inside her at last, he regained a little of his sanity. "Whitney…forgive me… I had to."

"I know." Her eyes blazed with passion as she bracketed his face with both hands and gazed up at him. "I'm glad you had to."

He gulped for air. "But the eggs will be ruined."

"I don't care."

"I gave you whisker burn. Your chin's red."

"I don't *care*." Releasing her grip on his face, she shoved her hands under the denim of his jeans and clutched his hips. "It's been two long weeks, Ty!"

He shuddered. "Believe me, I know how long it's been."

Her fingers flexed and she lifted her hips to align them more perfectly with his. "So let's make up for it. Give me what you've got, cowboy."

He sucked in a breath. "That's a promise." And he proceeded to make good on that promise as he poured days of frustration into every vigorous thrust. He'd driven for hours through a blizzard for this…and this… and dear God, *this*.

The sound of her breathless pleas as she urged him on inspired him to move faster and push deeper. He sought her heat again and again, pounding into her as if he could never get enough. He wouldn't last long at this pace, but neither would she. Already the quiver of her impending climax squeezed his aching cock.

He had to come, couldn't hold back. Not this time. Later he'd make long, slow love to her, but now…now she trembled beneath him. Her thighs shook and her body arched upward as her cries of release filled his ears. He let go, coming with such force that he nearly blacked out.

When his brain stopped twirling, he was relieved to discover that he hadn't collapsed onto her. By some miracle his arms hadn't given way even though the rest of his body felt as if a paving machine had rolled him flat.

He had no confidence he could keep that upright position for long, though.

Easing away from her, he managed to climb out of bed and stagger into the bathroom. When he returned, she lay exactly as he'd left her, her nightgown pushed to her waist and her thighs moist with lovemaking.

Turning on her side, she regarded him with slumberous eyes. The movement caused the hem of her nightgown to slide down and cover her thighs, but the heat in her gaze was enough to jump-start his pulse. Although she looked like a satisfied woman, she gave him the distinct impression she was willing to be satisfied again.

Her seductive smile only confirmed it. "Why don't you take off your clothes and come back to bed? We need to sleep, and then we need to do that again."

"Only slower."

She laughed softly and her cheeks grew pink. "If that's what you want."

"I do, but if we're going to stay here, I'd better go check the stove to see if anything's still on, like the eggs."

"Nothing's on."

"You're sure?"

"I shut everything off."

"When?"

"When I caught sight of you devouring that toast. Suddenly I wanted you so much I couldn't breathe."

He stared at her in disbelief. "I turned you on by eating *toast*?"

"You weren't just eating it. You were diving into it with reckless abandon." She took a deep breath and met his gaze. "That's how you make love to me, and it's… intoxicating."

There was no mistaking the hunger in her eyes and

Lord help him, he responded. Blood hummed through his veins and gathered in a predictable spot. He started unsnapping his shirt. "I still haven't shaved."

"Ask me if I care."

"A minute ago you mentioned something about sleeping." He dropped his shirt on top of his duffel and reached for the button on his jeans.

She glanced at the telltale bulge behind his fly. "You don't look sleepy."

He had to smile. "I'm not anymore." He unzipped slowly, easing past the briefs that were being seriously stretched by his thickening cock. "It seems I have to be nearly dead before I can sleep when you're around, especially when you look at me like that."

"Then I guess we're left with one option." Lazily she sat up and peeled off her nightgown. She did it slowly, revealing her glorious body inch by inch. At last she tossed the nightgown away and gazed at him. "I'll have to wear you out."

He froze, afraid if he moved a muscle he'd come. He'd always been in such a rush to have her that he'd never let himself take in the whole picture. Her cheeks weren't the only part flushed with desire. So were her shoulders, her arms, her breasts...

Ah, those breasts. He'd stroked them, licked them, kissed and nibbled them. But he hadn't really *looked*. He hadn't admired the tantalizing shape that so perfectly fit his cupped hands, or the pert tilt of her nipples and how the color deepened when she was aroused.

His glance moved lower, over her flat belly to the soft blond curls dampened by passion. His mouth watered as he remembered the thrill of tasting her. His fingertips tingled at the memory of caressing her silken thighs, the tender backs of her knees, her delicate ankles. Her toenails were painted pink. He hadn't noticed that before, either.

"Come to bed, Ty."

His gaze traveled slowly back up the length of her tempting body. Then he looked into her eyes as he shoved down his jeans and briefs. "Gonna wear me out, huh?"

"You say that like you think I can't."

"I don't know if you can or not." His pulse raced in anticipation as he climbed into bed. "But I'm more than willing to let you try."

15

As soon as Ty was in bed beside her, Whitney had him lie on his back. But as she was about to straddle his thighs and have her way with her tasty cowboy, she had an idea. "Stay there. I'll be right back." Climbing over him, she headed out of the bedroom.

"I thought you said everything was shut off?"

"It is," she called over her shoulder. "I'm just getting a couple of things." She returned with the can of whipped cream she'd planned to use for the cocoa and a large bath towel. "Scoot over so I can put a towel under you."

He followed her instructions. Once he was stretched out on the terry cloth, he stuffed a pillow behind his head. Then he watched her with a wicked gleam in his eye and a teasing smile. "I can't wait to see how this turns out."

"Me, either. I've never tried it."

"I see."

"Have you?" Before getting into bed, she took a condom out for later.

His chuckle was low and sexy. "I've had whipped cream before, if that's what you're asking."

"That's not what I'm asking." She'd never admit it to

him, but the combination of his beard and that smile reminded her of the calendar. They weren't the only factors, either. The man in the picture had looked as if he wouldn't hesitate to drive twelve hours through a snowstorm to make love to the woman he wanted.

The sedate lawyer she'd known in Cheyenne wouldn't have dreamed of doing something that impetuous and foolhardy. Or if he had, he'd bring along a laptop so he could also get some work done. Ty had brought only a change of clothes and some toiletries.

Maybe the blizzard and the threat of not seeing her had caused him to abandon his careful facade this weekend. After making love to him in the back of her Subaru she'd known he could do it. She just didn't know if the transformation would last.

That was why she'd wanted to take this relationship slow and easy. She'd wanted to give it room to grow at its own pace instead of rushing and perhaps ruining everything. Instead, they were marooned in this apartment, probably for another twelve hours, at least.

They wouldn't have work, friends or family to interrupt them. She had a feeling that forced proximity could permanently alter the dynamic. She couldn't begin to predict the outcome, but she could take advantage of the time to really get to know him. She'd allow him to know her, too. Then she'd let the chips fall where they may.

She tossed the condom on the far side of the bed.

He glanced at it. "Is that a before or after item?"

"After. When we get down to serious business."

"Just so you know, I have a seriously stiff—"

"I noticed." Standing beside him, she shook the can as she considered the possibilities. "Where to start, where to start."

"I have a suggestion."

"I'm sure you do, but this is my game." Holding the can, she slid in next to him. "After nearly ten years of working in a coffee shop, I know how to handle whipped cream."

"Then I'm in the hands of a professional?"

"Exactly. One who's perfectly qualified to try this at home. I can't think now why I never have."

"You were lacking the proper inspiration?"

She looked into his eyes and found the rake lurking there. "Could be." Easing one leg over his stomach, she lay belly to belly with her bottom nestled up against the seriously stiff anatomical feature he'd mentioned.

"I'm liking that." He grasped her hips and wedged himself in tighter. "Maybe we should forget about the whipped cream. If you'll just reach over and get that condom, I can—"

"Nope. Not yet." Although feeling his hard length pressed against her bottom was very erotic indeed. "Open your mouth."

"My mouth?" He started laughing. "I was so hoping you'd squirt it on my—"

"Maybe I will if you're a good boy. Open your mouth."

"Okay, but this is what we used to do as kids. I was expecting a more grown-up whipped cream adventure."

"It will be. Open up." When he finally obeyed, she squirted whipped cream into his mouth. Then she dived in with her tongue.

He caught on quick and they enjoyed the sweetest, messiest kiss, especially when the cream got all over his bristly chin. She did her best to lick it clean for him while they kissed and kissed some more, all the while giggling like fools.

Next she squirted some on her nipple, and he sucked so enthusiastically that she accidentally sprayed whipped cream into the hollow of his neck. "Stop." She disengaged her breast from his talented mouth.

"Don't want to." He cupped her breast. "Let me—"

"No, I have to lick up what I just sprayed on you."

"I thought you meant to do that." He squeezed her breast gently.

"No."

"Aren't you a pro?" His eyes sparkled with heat and mischief.

"Yes, but I can't control the nozzle when I'm trying not to come, so turn me loose so I can lick your throat."

"Okay, but my throat's not an erogenous zone."

"You don't know that. Maybe it is." Propped on her forearms, she began slurping up the rapidly melting whipped cream.

"That tickles."

"Hold still. I have to get it before it starts dribbling." She licked the side of his neck. Then for fun she nipped him.

"So now you're a vampire?"

"Maybe." She had cleaned up most of the whipped cream but she kept licking and nipping because his breathing had changed and his pulse beat faster. He might not think his throat was an erogenous zone, but she was about to prove him wrong.

"Mmm." The soft sound wasn't quite a moan, but it was close. He slipped both hands down to her bottom.

The urgent press of his fingertips told her he was getting into this. After nuzzling his throat some more, she created a small ring of whipped cream around each of his nipples. Then she proceeded to lick and nibble him there.

His murmured *damn* and his ragged breathing encouraged her to repeat the process. When at last she kissed her way back to his sticky mouth, he met her with an urgent groan and an eager tongue.

She lifted her head to gaze down at him. "Having fun?"

His gray eyes gleamed with pleasure. "More than you could ever guess."

"Good. Next stage."

"I hope I know what that is."

"You don't." Moving to one side, she ran a line of whipped cream from his breastbone to his navel.

He yelped. "God, that's cold."

"I'll warm you up." And she began lapping at his skin with long, lazy strokes of her tongue.

"Wow." He blew out a slow breath. "That's so… I didn't think I'd…"

"Like it?" she murmured against his damp skin.

"Yeah. All of it. I didn't realize that my skin…that I'm sensitive…everywhere."

The hint of vulnerability in his voice touched her. She'd launched into this as a sexy adventure, but it was about more than that. He'd let his guard down by allowing her to cover him in whipped cream and teach him things he hadn't known about himself. That kind of trust was precious.

He shuddered when she dipped her tongue into his navel and his cock twitched. She became aware that he'd clutched handfuls of the sheet and was hanging on tight. Time to get this show on the road. She'd meant to play around some more, but her emphasis had shifted. She wanted to love this beautiful man who'd opened up to her.

"Last stage," she said softly. Instead of spraying the whipped cream directly on him, she squirted it into her hand. Then she gently brushed it on his cock with the tips of her fingers before licking it away.

"Whitney." His voice sounded rusty. "I'm about to explode."

"That's okay."

"No it isn't. I want—" His breath hissed between his teeth as she continued to smear him with whipped cream. "You need to get...to get the condom."

"Not this time. This time it's all about you." She drew him into her mouth. Then she took him deeper and sucked hard.

He tensed and swore. Then with a helpless cry of surrender he came. She swallowed the salty essence of him as he gasped out more pithy swearwords. If her mouth hadn't been busy with other things, she would have smiled.

At last he dragged in a deep breath and let it out. "Come here," he murmured.

Gently releasing his warm cock, she scooted up beside him, propped her fist on his chest and rested her chin there. "You rang, sire?"

He combed his fingers through her hair as his gaze held hers. "I feel like a king. That was...incredible."

"Are you sure? Because you swore a lot."

The corners of his mouth tilted up. "That's so I wouldn't scream like a girl. I thought the top of my head was coming off."

"Really? It was that good?"

"Really. Nothing beats the sensation of thrusting deep inside you, but this... It's hard to describe but I just..."

"Let it happen?"

He chuckled softly. "Yeah, but I didn't have a choice, which made it even more amazing. You took the controls and I was done for."

"I wanted you to be done for." She was giddy with happiness.

"But now there's a lonely condom lying on your side of the bed." He brushed his thumb over her cheek. "You wouldn't have taken it out of the drawer if you weren't planning for us to use it."

"I was, but then I changed my mind."

"Why?"

"Because I wanted to do something special for you. I wanted to make you happy."

"You made me very happy."

Her long-range plan had been to have great sex followed by snuggling and falling asleep, but the whipped cream had created a small glitch. "I got you kind of sticky, though."

"I'm sure. Maybe I should take a quick shower."

"Too much trouble." A shower would only wake him up. "I'll get a warm washcloth and a hand towel."

"Don't bother. I'll shower." He started to get up.

She put a restraining hand on his chest. "My game, my rules." She scrambled out of bed. "I'll be back in a jiffy."

"If you think we're going to cuddle and fall asleep, you have another think coming. I'm not sleeping until we've used that condom."

"That's fine." She had his number, now. If she bathed him with warm water and wrapped him in her arms, he'd be out like a light. He needed sleep and so did she. They had a big day ahead of them.

When she returned with the washcloth and a fresh towel, he was obviously battling to keep his eyes open.

Nevertheless, he reached for the washcloth. "I can do it."

"Let me. I want to."

When he gave in, she knew the battle was won. Working quickly, she wiped away the sticky residue and stroked the soft towel over every damp place she created.

"Feels nice," he murmured, his eyelids drifting closed.

"Good." She finished up and took the washcloth and towel back to the bathroom. By the time she returned, his eyes were closed. Smiling, she pulled the covers over him. Then she walked around the bed, put the condom on her nightstand and turned out the light.

As she climbed into bed, she debated whether to snuggle against him. But that might wake him, and she wanted him to rest. Turning her back to him so that she'd resist the temptation to watch him sleep, she closed her eyes.

Moments later a strong arm came around her and pulled her into the curve of his body. He was hard again. "Okay, we won't use it now if you'd rather not." His breath was warm in her ear. "I admit I'm a pretty sad specimen who definitely needs a shave."

"That's not the issue. You need sleep far more than you need a shave. Or more sex."

"You need sleep, too." He cupped her breast almost casually, his fingers flexing. "Good night." His cock pressed against the curve of her backside. "We'll touch base in the morning."

She found that comment hysterical. "Touch base? Is that something you say to clients?"

He chuckled. "Sometimes. What should I say? We'll knock boots in the morning?"

"It *is* morning, you crazy cowboy."

"Well, there you go. It's time to knock boots. Hand me the condom. I've figured out how to do this so I won't scratch you any more than I already have."

"You're certifiable." But the whipped cream incident had left her hot and achy, and now he was suggesting that he wanted to take care of that problem. "Good thing I like that in a person." She handed the condom packet over her shoulder. "Here you go."

"Thanks. Appreciate it."

"Why is this all sounding like a business deal?"

"It'll get intensely personal in just a second." After a rustle of foil, he bracketed her hips with his large hands. "From me to you, sweet Whitney." Holding her steady, he took her slowly from behind.

And oh, it was glorious. Once he'd filled her and had begun to pump with an easy rhythm, he slid one hand over her hip and through her curls. His knowing fingers caressed her as he rocked gently back and forth.

Compared to the frantic coupling they'd had in the past, this seemed tame, almost civilized. And yet before she quite realized it, her body clenched. Without warning she flowed into a dazzling spiral of an orgasm that seemed to go on and on because he kept moving, kept thrusting. Moaning and whimpering, she lost herself in the beauty of it.

Then he shifted his angle and drove in deeper. His fingers spread over her, cupping her and holding her steady as his thighs slapped hard against her bottom. His strokes had found a trigger point and she tightened again, wailing as a second climax crashed over her. With a loud bellow he pushed up and in, his cock pulsing deep inside her body.

As she lay there panting and dazed, he withdrew as gently as he'd entered her. Leaning forward, he combed her hair aside and placed a soft kiss on her shoulder. "Don't go away. I still want to cuddle."

Well, now. So much for thinking she was in control. But she had to admit that she liked knowing he would take that control back when it suited him. She could never be happy with a man who allowed her to be in charge all the time.

The jury was still out, but she thought maybe she could be happy with Ty. They still had a whole lot of things to talk about, specifically his parents and her sister, but if they could work through that, they might have a shot.

The whisper of his footsteps on the carpet made her heart beat faster. She liked having him around and wouldn't mind turning it into a regular thing. But that was another problem, a five-hour problem.

He climbed into bed. "If you're asleep, don't mind me." Once again he wrapped an arm around her and pulled her close.

She started laughing. "*Don't mind me?* What the hell is that supposed to mean? If I had been asleep, I wouldn't be anymore after being manhandled."

"I knew you weren't asleep and you like being manhandled." He tucked her in closer, his hand cupping her breast again.

"I could've been asleep. It's possible."

"Nah, you weren't. You were lying there thinking about things."

"Like what?" She was fascinated that he'd guessed that.

"Like us, and where this is all going."

Her breath caught. "Where is it all going?"

"I don't know." He nestled against her. "We'll talk about it after we get some sleep."

"Okay." She relaxed against him, comforted in the knowledge that she wasn't the only one thinking about the future.

16

Ty woke to soft gray light and Whitney's smooth backside pressed against the woody of the century. On top of that, he was starving to death. How could he be so hungry and still have an erection hard enough to drive nails? Mother Nature could be cruel.

Whitney's steady breaths told him she was zonked out and he wasn't about to disturb her sleep if he could help it. That ruled out solving one of his problems, but he might be able to handle the other one without waking her. He had enough light to see so he wouldn't trip over his duffel this time.

He slipped away from Whitney's temptingly warm body and eased out of bed. Then he waited, breath held. She stirred and murmured something before her even breaths resumed.

Picking up his clothes and exiting the room without making noise was a piece of cake. After living with three boys in a cabin at Thunder Mountain, he'd learned to be quiet when others were sleeping. Guys who couldn't manage that usually found their bunks sabotaged the next time they climbed in.

He carefully closed the bedroom door and waited until

he was in the kitchen before he pulled on his clothes. The kitchen window was iced over so he couldn't see what was going on outside. But walking naked through her apartment had taken care of his woody, and the prospect of putting something in his stomach focused his mind on a topics other than sex. God, he was hungry.

Not wasting time fastening the snaps on his shirt, he lifted the lid on the pan of eggs. They looked shriveled but they might not taste too bad. He found a fork and stabbed a chunk of the dried-out eggs.

Ugh. He chewed and swallowed because he wasn't going to spit them into the garbage. That would be gross. If he'd had no other alternative he would have forced himself to eat everything in the pan. Instead he grabbed the loaf of cinnamon bread.

Briefly he considered toasting it and decided not to. He didn't want to take a chance that the scent of cinnamon toast would rouse her. Or the aroma of coffee. After making that stupid statement about never wanting coffee again, he wanted some right now.

He spread peanut butter and cherry jam on two slices of bread and slapped them together. Then he bit into the sandwich and moaned. Once on his second one, he gazed with longing at her espresso machine.

Even if he could operate it, which was unlikely, he'd make noise and the smell of brewing coffee would fill the apartment. Or the smell of burned coffee because he'd screwed it up. That would be worse. He rummaged through the cupboards in the vain hope of finding instant coffee, but of course she wouldn't have any. She was a professional.

He finished off the loaf of bread and took the spare one out of the freezer for when she woke up. She had more eggs in the refrigerator and he looked forward to eventually eating some that weren't petrified. But he wasn't going to cook them while she was still asleep. He quietly scraped the old ones into the garbage but decided against scouring out the pan. Instead he ran a little water in it.

The cocoa had a film over it. It should still be good, though. Too bad he couldn't warm it up, but then he'd risk filling the apartment with the scent of hot chocolate. He checked to make sure she had more milk before skimming the film off and stirring the mixture.

He filled a mug and drank it cold. Not bad. He refilled the mug and polished off the rest of it. Then he remembered the can of whipped cream that was still in the bedroom. They could make more cocoa, but he doubted the unrefrigerated whipped cream would survive to squirt another day.

Just as well. He'd never look at another can of whipped cream without thinking of how Whitney had reduced him to a hot mess of sexual neediness. She knew some things about him now that he hadn't known about himself. The feel of her tongue against his skin had touched off a primitive and unrecognized yearning.

He wanted to be with her as often as they both could manage it. Not living in the same city would complicate that because he probably couldn't make the ten-hour round trip more than once or twice a month. Their schedules didn't match up well, either. He put in a five-day week and she often had to work nights and weekends. But those were details. They'd figure it out.

He wandered barefoot into the living room with its unlit tree and a pile of wrapped presents underneath. Crouching beside the tree, he turned the timer from Auto to On and the lights glowed. Better.

He glanced at the wrapped packages, all with ribbons

and tags. One said To Grammy Jones, Love, Whitty. So she had a nickname. And gifts for a whole slew of relatives. The back of her Subaru would be loaded up like Santa's sleigh.

His parents' tree used to be crowded with presents, too, even though the family had consisted of three people. His mom loved Christmas and thought everyone should have lots to open on Christmas morning. So he and his dad made sure that she had plenty of gifts, too.

They'd shopped together, with him spending his allowance and whatever money he'd earned shoveling snow and mowing lawns, and his dad charging her gifts to his personal credit card to keep the purchases secret. Together they'd meander down the aisles of the local bookstore because his mother had been a big reader.

But they'd stop at the jewelry store, too, because his dad loved getting something pretty, and then they'd browse the toy store looking for silly things to make her laugh. The light-up Slinky had been a real hit. She'd set up time trials for the Slinky's progress down the stairs. He couldn't remember her smiling face but he could picture the Slinky undulating down from the second floor.

His throat ached as he stood and walked away from the tree. For one awful moment he was angry with Whitney because she still had all of that in her life. Taking a deep breath, he let the anger go.

He'd had to learn that trick or he would have been eaten up with anger and jealousy. The waves of anger didn't come over him so much anymore, but that was partly because he didn't dwell on what he'd lost. No point, especially if it stirred up emotions he needed to keep in check.

"Good morning."

Swallowing the lump in his throat, he turned toward

the hallway where she stood wearing her granny gown and looking pink and rumpled. She'd piled her hair on top of her head and secured it in that mysterious way only women seemed capable of. His heart lifted at the sight of her and he smiled. "Good morning."

"I didn't hear you get up."

"That was on purpose." He walked toward her and cupped her face gently in both hands. How he loved looking into those warm brown eyes. "I desperately want to kiss you, but I'm not going to until I've shaved this porcupine off my chin. I gave you whisker burn and I'm deeply sorry."

She grinned at him. "Well, I'm not sorry for a single thing, so there." She stroked his cheek. "If you let your beard grow, it would get softer. Beards are making a comeback, you know."

"Not at my firm. The senior partners have made that very clear."

"Okay, then." She sighed. "But it was fun to think about." She rubbed her knuckles over his prickly chin. "What have you been doing while I slept the morning away?"

Letting old memories swamp him, never a good thing. "Ate the rest of that loaf of bread and turned on the Christmas lights. I think a blizzard demands Christmas lights all day, don't you?"

"Absolutely. I'm going to make coffee, but maybe you still don't want—"

"Oh, I want, especially if it's prepped by a professional."

That made her laugh. "My equipment's not as good as what I have at the shop, but I can whip up a mean latte if that interests you."

"Very much. I'll shave while you're doing that. Do I have time to shower?"

"I suppose." She gazed up at him. "But I don't have a huge hot water tank."

"Oh, then I'll wait until after you shower. No problem."

Her seductive smile was back. "Or…we could have some coffee, and maybe some eggs, and then…we could shower together."

A potent image of water sluicing over her breasts and running in rivulets down her thighs was all he needed to rev his engines. He tilted her face up to his. "Or we could forget the coffee."

"It'll be more fun after we've had coffee. We'll be more awake."

"I'm awake. Parts of me are *really* awake, if you know what I mean."

"Oh, man, do I ever." Her voice was husky as she met his gaze. Then she grasped his hand and turned her head to lick his palm.

He sucked in a breath.

With another smile that fried his brain, she slipped away from him. "Go shave before we end up rolling around on the floor. You wouldn't want to give me rug burn, too." Turning, she walked into the kitchen with a sway to her hips.

"There's no rug in the kitchen," he called after her. "Just sayin'."

"No, but the floor is very hard."

"That's not the only thing."

"Go shave, cowboy!"

Laughing, he walked down the hall to fetch his shaving kit. Less than ten minutes later, he was back in the kitchen in time for her to hand him a mug with froth decorating the top.

"Your latte, but I'm afraid it's not peppermint."

"No worries. The personal service makes it special." He took the mug and raised it in her direction. "Here's to your continued success at Rangeland Roasters."

"I admit the future looks bright for the Sheridan location." She took a sip. "Ah. Nothing like a little jolt of caffeine to start the day."

He could think of another way that would be sweeter, but the opportunity had been lost for this particular day. He drank some. "This is really good. You obviously love coffee."

"I adore it. I have ever since I was about five and my mom let me have some laced with a lot of milk and some sugar. I've told her this career is all her doing. Hey, do you want some eggs? I have another frying pan so we don't even have to sandblast the remains from the other one."

"That sounds great. But I'm going to help you."

"Then I'll give you the bowl and the whisk. I'll melt butter in the pan and drink coffee."

"Deal." Spending time with her was so relaxing, probably because she had a gift for easy companionship. In minutes they had plates full of scrambled eggs to go with their coffee. They decided to let the bread thaw some more before trying to toast it.

He sat across from her at the little kitchen table. Their Chinese meal when he'd introduced her to the use of chopsticks seemed like years ago. He'd made a half-assed attempt to control his rapid slide into total commitment. He hadn't succeeded and now he was in up to his neck.

"What about you?" She scooped up a forkful of eggs. "What inspired you to go into contract law?"

"My mom." And there they were, back in the danger zone that could blast this cozy setup into a million pieces. But maybe not. He'd give this discussion a try.

"How so?"

"That was her specialty." If he had a nickel for every time he'd wished she could be here to see how well he was doing with it, he'd be a very wealthy man.

"What a nice thing, to follow in her footsteps."

He looked into her eyes, drawing strength from her calm expression. "Like I said, I inherited her photographic memory, so it seemed like a logical choice."

"And maybe an emotional one, too?" Her voice was soft and nonthreatening.

Yet the question poked at a sore spot and he tensed. "I suppose it was." He soldiered on. "I spent all those years hearing about what she did, and it sounded cool to me. In some ways, contracts are the backbone of our society. A handshake used to be enough, but today we require a contract for almost anything we consider significant." It was something she'd told him long ago and he'd always remembered it. But he'd never repeated it before.

"That's absolutely true." She continued to eat as if they were having a casual conversation. "How about your dad? What did he do?"

"He sold appliances. Refrigerators, stoves, stuff like that." And he had stories about his customers that would have Ty and his mom rolling on the floor. God, he missed those stories. The hollow place in the pit of his stomach grew larger.

This was why he didn't talk about his parents. Rosie had tried to get him to do that and he'd refused. The foster boys at Thunder Mountain had asked a few questions but hadn't pressed him for answers. In contrast to their stories, his life had probably sounded pretty good to them, at least up to the point where it had all ended.

"I'll bet you had top-of-the-line equipment in your house."

"Yep." According to the lawyer who'd handled the estate, the primo stove, refrigerator, washer and dryer had made the house easier to sell. He'd mentioned it to Ty as if he'd thought that would be comforting.

"I have an uncle who sells appliances. His sales technique cracks me up. He shows customers an appliance and then says *do you want it or not*? No subtlety whatsoever. He's the top salesperson in his region."

"Whitney…" He tried to think how to say something that wouldn't sound offensive and ruin what he hoped would be a nice day together. A nice life together, in fact. "I don't talk about them very much, so if you don't mind, I'd—"

"I've noticed." Her gaze was direct. "But I really like you. I'd love to know more about what made you the amazing man you are today."

He pushed his plate away. "I wish I could just talk about them, but it's hard for me. I can see why you wouldn't get that, though."

"Try me."

"It's like I've had two lives, one before the plane crash and one after. The one that came after is an open book. Ask me anything. We can talk about Rosie and Herb, my best friend, Brant, life on the ranch, whatever. That's a big part of who I am."

She shoved her plate aside, too. "Of course it is. I've spent time with Rosie and she's a force to be reckoned with. I'm willing to bet that without her, you would be in a whole other place."

He sighed in relief. This he could talk about. "I would

have ended up in a juvenile detention center. I was a violent kid prone to rages. I broke things, including noses if somebody got in my face."

"That's so hard for me to imagine. You're one of the gentlest guys I've ever met."

"Not when I'm angry, and I was very angry. The world had dealt me a bad hand and it wasn't fair. I wanted to get even."

"I can understand that."

He gazed at her and thought of all the Christmas gifts grouped around the tree. He pictured Christmas Eve and Christmas Day with her extended family. Joy and love would surround her, had surrounded her, for her entire life.

"It's natural to say you understand." He said it kindly because he didn't want to be mean or cruel. She'd had a blessed life that had made her into a wonderful person who wished only the best things for everyone. He cherished that. "But I don't think you do. I don't know how you could."

"You might be surprised."

The slight edge to her voice put him on alert. "What do you mean?"

"I've been trying to decide when I should tell you this. We potentially could spend the whole day together, so saying it before high noon is probably stupid. It could backfire."

His heart thumped crazily in his chest. "But you've launched into it, so you have to tell me."

"I know." She sighed. "I didn't mean to bring it up now. Or maybe I did. I was the one who started asking questions about your folks."

"Go on." He braced himself. Unfortunately life had taught him to be prepared for the worst.

"Okay, before I say anything more, this is not at all like your situation. It's totally different and comparisons should never be made. However." She took a shaky breath. "I have firsthand experience with a single incident splitting a life in half."

His palms were sweating and he barely managed to get the question out. "What happened?"

"A month after my twin sister, Selena, and I turned sixteen, she was killed in a car accident."

He stared at her and tried to wrap his mind around what she'd said. "Your twin sister?" Pressure built in his chest.

"Yes."

"Why...why am I just hearing about this now?"

"Because... I didn't want..." She looked away. "You've been through so much. Telling you about Selena seemed like a cheap way to bond with you, like I was using her death to get closer."

"Dear God." He was out of his chair and pulling her out of hers. "I would never think that." His heart ached for her. He'd never had a sibling, but he had foster brothers. To lose one was unthinkable. He gathered her into his arms and cradled her head against his chest. A sister. And a twin, which seemed even worse. "I'm so sorry."

"But you need to understand." She lifted her head and looked into his eyes. "I've accepted what happened. I've come out the other side. It's okay."

"It's never okay." But he knew what would make it better, at least for a little while. "Come with me." Taking her hand, he led her into the bedroom.

17

WHITNEY UNDERSTOOD TY's impulse to make love. He didn't believe that she'd truly accepted Selena's death and he wanted to comfort her in the best way he knew. Maybe it didn't matter whether he believed her or not. Her confession had probably stirred up his own feelings of grief and he might be the one in need of comfort.

But if he thought he was doing this for her, she'd take that as a gift of love. His reaction to hearing about Selena told her more clearly than words that he'd come to love her. As she had come to love him.

If she hadn't admitted it before, she knew it now. Instead of squirming with impatience as she watched him undress, she waited for him with a warm glow of anticipation. She wanted to hold him and feel his skin against hers as they communicated with sweet touches and soft murmurs. She cherished the privilege of being in his arms just as she knew he cherished the privilege of being in hers.

Looking into his warm gray eyes as he climbed into bed and moved over her, she glimpsed a depth of emotion that hadn't been there before. He didn't have to say it. His tender kiss and his gentleness as he entered her demonstrated how much she meant to him.

He loved her with sure, steady strokes. Gradually the sadness that had lingered in his eyes gave way to the joy of giving.

She hugged him close and poured all the love she felt into her gaze. "Thank you."

"My pleasure." He smiled. "Although it's your pleasure I'm after."

"I know." She lifted her hips to meet the thrusts that wound her body tighter each time he pumped. "And you're...achieving it."

"Thought so."

"Can you feel it?"

"Yeah." His voice roughened. "And I can see it in your eyes."

And do you see the love there, too? "Come with me."

He shook his head. "As someone else said..." He took a ragged breath. "This is all about you."

"Then come with me." She gripped his flexing buttocks and pushed up against him with a soft moan. "Because that's my favorite."

Awareness flashed in his eyes. "Mine, too." He held her gaze as he rocked his hips faster. "Mine, too, sweet Whitney."

She gulped for air as her climax hovered nearer. "Deal?"

"Deal." And he bore down, his gray eyes darkening to the color of storm clouds. Then he paused, gasping. "Ready?"

"Oh, yeah." She pressed her fingertips into his bunching muscles.

"Then here we go." With a low groan he drove home one last time.

She surrendered to the power of that final thrust. As her body responded with an explosion of pure pleasure, he let out a hoarse cry and shuddered against her. The undulating waves of her climax, blending with the steady pulsing of his, filled her with such joy that tears spilled from the corners of her eyes.

His fingers trembled as he wiped them away. "I'm so, so sorry."

"Those are…" She paused to clear her throat. "Those are happy tears."

He didn't look convinced.

"They are." She rubbed his back, sweaty despite the coolness of the room. "Making love with you is so wonderful that I get a little choked up."

He leaned down and kissed her softly. "Well, now you've told me about your sister, so we don't have to talk about that anymore today."

"I don't mind if we talk about her." She could tell from his doubtful expression that he thought she was putting on a brave front for his sake. "Honestly, I don't. I wasn't crying over her. I was crying because I—" She almost said *because I love you* but quickly thought better of it. She didn't want that declaration to be mixed up with talk about Selena. Then he wouldn't believe her about that, either. "I really was happy, not sad."

"Okay." He didn't add *if you say so* but he might as well have. He was definitely humoring her. "Is that shared shower offer still open?"

"Sure is."

He leaned down and kissed her again. "Then I'll meet you in the bathroom."

AT FIRST THEY played like kids in the shower, throwing wet washcloths and generally making a mess. Then they played like adults, using their mouths and tongues and the spray of water. They were both clean and satisfied by the time they dried off and mopped up the floor.

Whitney had had a blast, but she also couldn't help wondering if Ty was still trying to cheer her up. He seemed to be in caretaking mode and insisted on drying her hair. So after they were both dressed, she handed him the brush and the hairdryer and he sat on the futon while she sat on the floor between his knees.

She enjoyed the pampering even though he could use some practice at blow-drying a woman's hair. But she couldn't help thinking that he was treating her like someone who'd suffered a horrible shock. She had, but she'd worked through the bad times and every year was a little easier. She'd like to talk with him about that, in fact. It could be very important if they were planning to keep seeing each other.

After he finished with her hair, they ate peanut butter sandwiches for lunch and drank more coffee while they checked the road conditions. Nothing was moving except the snowplows, so they went through her stash of board games and ended up playing Sorry! on her living room rug.

The game was simple enough that it was only fun if the participants were ruthless. Ty wasn't ruthless. He pretended that he hadn't seen the moves that would have allowed him to beat her.

She wasn't buying it. At the end of the second game, she picked up the cards and held on to them instead of shuffling. "You're the person with the photographic memory, so either your head's not in the game or you're letting me win on purpose."

He smiled at her. "Maybe I'm just trying to butter

you up so you'll have sex with me once more before I have to leave."

"You don't have to let me win a board game to get me naked, Ty." She put down the deck.

"Really? Excellent." He started gathering up the pieces. "Let's bag this program and—"

"Hang on, there, cowboy."

"What?" He glanced up.

"I need to ask you something." She knew this next move was risky, but in another hour or so he'd be gone. She'd never have a better opportunity to broach the subject, now that he knew about Selena and they wouldn't be interrupted. "Aren't you the least bit curious about how losing my twin sister affected my life?"

Panic flashed briefly in his eyes, the only emotion that he showed before he closed down and looked away. "I have a pretty good idea."

"Do you?"

He continued to gather pieces and tuck them in the box. "At first there's the kind of pain you think you can't stand, but somehow you do, and if you're lucky, you find the strength to deal with it. It might have been a little easier having your family around, but I wouldn't want to make that assumption. I had Rosie and Herb and it still sucked." He closed up the box and looked at her. "Does that about sum it up?"

She pushed the box away and inched closer so their knees touched. Then she took one of his big hands in both of hers. "For you, maybe." She looked into his eyes. "Not for me."

He sucked in a breath. "It was worse?"

"No, it was better."

"Then I'm glad for you, Whitney, really glad. The thought of you suffering…" He cupped her cheek with his free hand. "Until you told me about Selena, I pictured you as a golden girl living a golden life, and I was happy about that." He sighed. "Mostly. I had a moment of jealousy when I saw all those presents under your tree, but I got over it."

She gave silent thanks for his honesty on that point. It was something to hang on to. "And how do you think of me now?"

"As a fellow survivor, I guess."

"Okay." She started to say more.

"But I don't see the need to talk about it," he added quickly, as if to cut off further discussion. "Just like soldiers don't talk about the battles they've fought in. Better to just forget about it and go on. That's my motto."

This might be tougher than she'd thought. "I respect that position and maybe sometimes it's the only answer. But in my case—and yours—I don't happen to agree with it."

"I'm beginning to see that."

She chose her words carefully. "I don't believe that we can just bury our memories. In my opinion, they're still there, and if we don't get them out and dust them off, they can calcify and block off the good stuff."

"You sound like Rosie."

"That can't be a bad thing."

"It isn't." He stroked her cheek with his thumb. "I know you're trying to help just like she did, and I appreciate that. But what good would it do to talk about my dead parents? Talking doesn't bring them back."

"But it does!" She gripped his hand tighter because she felt him mentally pulling away. "When I'm at home with my folks, we talk about Selena. Not constantly, but if one of us thinks of her or remembers something she used to do, we share those thoughts. It helps so much. You have no idea."

"You're right." The warmth in his eyes disappeared and for the first time there was an edge to his voice. "I have no idea because I don't have your situation."

"I realize that, but—"

"Whitney, can we not do this?" He combed her hair back from her forehead. "Think about it. You have an entire group of people, family and friends, who remember your sister and are willing to share memories. That's great, but I don't. The only people who knew my parents really well have moved away and I don't know how to find them. Besides, their memories and mine would be very different."

"That doesn't mean you shouldn't share those memories with someone."

"Like who? Some therapist? No, thank you."

"No." She took a deep breath. "Like me."

"But you didn't even know them."

"Then tell me about them! Make them live for me!"

"I can't." Defeat laced his words. "I can't even remember what they looked like."

She gasped in disbelief. "But you have a photographic—"

"Yes, and when it comes to them, it's totally disabled. I've never told anyone that, so I'd appreciate it if you wouldn't, either."

"I won't, but Ty, you must have actual pictures of them somewhere." Unless he'd destroyed them. Her heart ached at the possibility that he might have in a moment of rage.

"I have the family albums in a sealed box."

Thank God. "We could go over them together. I promise you it will help."

He looked at her for several long seconds. "You don't understand what you're asking of me."

"You don't understand what you're giving up."

"Sadly, I think I do." Sliding his hand free, he stood. "I should probably check the road conditions."

She scrambled to her feet, her stomach churning. "Ty, it would be easier than you think."

He turned to her, his expression resigned. "I've spent fourteen years getting to the point where I don't want to hit something when I think of that plane crash. You're proposing that I tear down all those defenses and take a chance I'll be right back where I started. I'm not doing it."

"But then it's as if the first half of your life never happened! You can't tell me that's what you want."

"Yes I can. That's exactly what I want. It works for me."

She had trouble breathing. "But not for us," she murmured.

"No, not for us." His glance was tender. "But that was always a long shot, considering the distance between us."

She fought the urge to run into his arms and try to talk him out of his stubborn stance. But if she went to him and he rejected her, it would make the pain a hundred times worse. "Five hours isn't that much."

"I wasn't talking about the miles." He walked into the kitchen and picked up his phone from the counter where he'd left it earlier.

This couldn't be happening. Surely they wouldn't break up after some of the happiest hours of her life— and of his, too, she'd bet. But she'd known from the moment she'd begun to push him that he might push back.

She could try to backpedal, but damn it, this was important. She loved him, which meant she wanted to know whether he'd joined Cub Scouts or played baseball or built a tree house. She couldn't imagine being with someone whose entire childhood was a blank slate. And that he'd choose to keep it that way.

He walked out of the kitchen with his phone still in his hand. "The roads are okay. I should be fine from here to Cheyenne."

No, he wouldn't be fine. He would be an emotional mess who shouldn't be behind the wheel. "Stay here tonight," she said. "Call your office and explain that you don't want to risk driving back. You must have vacation days or sick days you haven't used."

"I do." His smile was sad. "But that will only make things tougher on both of us. You want something from me that I can't give. Let's cut our losses before this becomes any more painful than it already is."

"Ty, are you sure that I'm asking the impossible? Because from where I stand, it doesn't seem that way. This is something we could work at a little bit at a time. I'm not suggesting that you pour out your life story in one fell swoop."

"Like I said, easy for you to say, risky for me to do. I've plastered and spackled over the gaping holes in my story, and if I start scraping that patch job away, the whole structure might collapse."

"No, it won't." She took a step closer. "I'd be there to keep that from happening."

"You might want to be, but we live in different towns."

He had a point. Electronic communication could only accomplish so much. If she encouraged him to embrace his memories and that created issues for him, a cyber-hug wasn't going to do him much good.

He sighed. "How about we skip the drama, wish each other well and go our separate ways?"

The idea made her feel like throwing up. "Is that what you want?"

"What I want isn't possible, so let's not go there."

"At least tell me."

His gray eyes gleamed in defiance. "All right, here goes the impossible wish list. I wish my parents were alive because you'd love them and they'd love you. I want us to miraculously live in the same town so that neither of us has to give up our job. And as long as we're talking miracles, I want my parents to be alive but I also want to be a part of Thunder Mountain Ranch, because I'm crazy about my brothers and Rosie and Herb."

She swallowed. "Not everything on that list is impossible."

"All of it is impossible except the Thunder Mountain part. I don't know what magical world you're living in, but in my world my parents are still dead and you and I live in different cities and love our jobs. We need to give it up, Whitney. Some things are not meant to be."

"You sound as if you really believe that."

"It's hard-won wisdom." He drew in a shaky breath. "I'll go pack up my stuff." Turning, he walked down the hallway toward her bedroom.

Whitney stood in the middle of the living room and waited for him to come back out. Surely going back to the place where they'd shared so much passion and love, definitely love, would cause him to change his mind. She'd never had such a strong connection to a lover. She knew he hadn't, either, because she'd seen the emotion shining in his eyes. He wouldn't just leave.

But when he walked into the living room wearing his coat and hat and carrying his duffel, she knew that he would do exactly that. His face had lost all expression. It was like looking at a stranger.

He swallowed, the only sign that maybe he didn't have himself completely under control. "Goodbye, Whitney."

"So you're really going to do this." It was less a question and more a statement of disbelief.

"Obviously I'm not the right guy. I need to get out of your life so you can find him."

She didn't know what to say to that. She'd offered him her heart. Maybe not in so many words, but he had to know. She'd never fallen this hard for someone and his rejection hurt like hell.

"Whitney, don't look at me like that." His mask of indifference slipped a little and his voice softened. "This is for the best. You'll realize that eventually."

She drew in a ragged breath. "It might be for the best if you're determined to wall off a huge part of yourself. If that's your final word on the subject, then you're not the right guy." Her throat tightened. "But if you ever change your mind—"

"I won't."

Stupid man. "You probably won't, but if you ever do, you know where to find me." She clenched her fists until her nails bit into her palms. She would not reach for him.

He nodded. "Okay." And he turned and left.

She didn't move. Instead, ever the optimist, she stood there praying that he'd get partway down the hall and realize that he'd just abandoned his chance to live a whole life. For the rest of the day and well into the long, cold night, she kept expecting her intercom to buzz or her phone to ring. This was the man who'd driven through a blizzard to be with her. If he gave himself time to analyze that crazy trip, he might figure out why he'd made it.

Life had forced them both below the surface where they'd had to face grim reality at a very young age. Something in his psyche must have recognized the depth of emotion in hers and they'd bonded on a soul-deep level. No wonder their lovemaking had been so intense.

With a bond that strong, how could he imagine hiding a whole section of his life from her? Yet he'd been doing it with everyone else for years, including his beloved Rosie. Maybe he was capable of living like that, and if so, she really was better off without him.

As the days passed with no word from her stubborn cowboy, she finally admitted to Rosie one day that they weren't together anymore. Rosie didn't look happy about that. Then she must have passed the word to the others, because Phil, Damon, Lexi and Cade came by the shop soon after.

Lexi and Phil each gave her a hug and whispered that Ty was an idiot. Cade and Damon didn't say a whole lot, probably out of loyalty to their brother. But they ordered bigger cups of coffee than usual and left generous tips in the jar. At least losing Ty didn't mean she'd lost the connection to everyone at Thunder Mountain, which was comforting.

Gradually she began to accept that she'd fallen for the wrong guy. Worse yet, they'd broken up during the holidays, a time of love and good cheer. She worked extra hard to catch the Christmas spirit because she loved this time of year and she'd be damned if Ty was going to spoil it for her.

But instead of catching the Christmas spirit, she caught a cold. As she sniffled her way through the last couple of days before leaving for Cheyenne, she looked forward to having her mom baby her with chicken soup and back rubs. The excitement of Thanksgiving weekend with Ty had convinced her that she'd have a joyous holiday this year. But apparently she was in for a crappy one.

18

Ty CONSIDERED NOT driving up to Sheridan for Christmas, but he'd promised Rosie, so here he was on Christmas Eve, almost at the turnoff to the ranch. Good thing Brant would be there. Ty could use some of Brant's easygoing personality right now.

Brant wouldn't pester him about the breakup. Brant didn't even know Whitney, although knowing her wouldn't have changed his attitude. He was strictly a live-and-let-live kind of guy.

If Ty had announced he'd found the perfect woman, Brant would have been happy for him. But if Ty mentioned the breakup while they were here, Brant would probably shrug and say there were more fish in the sea. He wasn't into drama.

Rosie, on the other hand, was a worrier who believed each of her boys needed the love of a good woman. Until recently Ty had been happy to agree with her.

But in the past couple of weeks he'd had to face facts. He'd found a good woman and he'd had to let her go. He'd come closer to a commitment with Whitney than with anyone he'd dated, and that was why she'd started asking about his past.

What was more, she'd had every right to do that. So would anyone considering a serious relationship with him. For some reason he hadn't figured that out before, but now he realized that ultimately his choice was between digging up his buried past or staying single.

Contemplating that crummy realization had put a real crimp in his holiday cheer. Worse, he missed Whitney with an ache that refused to go away no matter how hard he worked or how many games of racquetball he played with his office buddies. Thoughts of her, both the sexy kind and the sweet kind, popped into his head on a depressingly regular basis. He dreamed about her every damned night. In spite of himself, he lived for those dreams.

He arrived at the ranch house at dusk, after the Christmas lights running across the roofline had come on. The last time he'd seen those lights he'd been with Whitney on their way to a celebration.

She'd be in Cheyenne by now, which was a good thing. If she'd stayed in Sheridan for Christmas he might not have been able to keep from going over there. She wouldn't have, though. Family was important to her and she'd be tucked into her old bedroom at her folks' house tonight.

He'd be out in the cabin he and Brant used to share with a couple of other guys. The bunks and desks might be different, but the cabin still had the power to bring back memories, the kind he could deal with. Too bad those memories wouldn't be enough to satisfy Whitney.

After parking his truck next to Brant's, he headed for the house carrying his duffel and a large shopping bag full of gifts. Brant must have been watching for him because he came out in his shirtsleeves grinning like a little kid. Or a big kid. The expression *a bear of a man* fit Brant to a *T*.

He slung a beefy arm around Ty's shoulders and hustled him into the house. "Mom will be happier than a puppy with a new chew toy when she lays eyes on you. We saw on the news there was a pileup on the highway. She tried calling your phone and when you didn't answer, well, you know how she gets."

"Didn't hear the phone. What pileup?" His brain went on tilt. "Northbound or southbound?"

"Both. A tractor-trailer jackknifed north of Casper and with the roads being icy, it was a mess. You didn't see anything?"

"Nope." Dear God, was Whitney okay? "Must have happened after I drove through there." *Please let her be okay.*

Brant chuckled. "You always were a lucky bastard." He opened the door and ushered Ty through it. "Let the rejoicing begin! The honorable Tyrone Slater is in the building!"

"Thank God!" Rosie rushed out of the kitchen and hugged him so tight he almost dropped the bag of gifts. "Why didn't you answer your phone?"

"Sorry. I can't always hear it, especially if I have music on."

Herb came over for his hug. "Glad you didn't end up in that rodeo, son. I honestly hate to see anyone out driving on Christmas Eve. Seems like a recipe for disaster."

"It sure is." His foster mom twisted her wedding band, a definite sign she was nervous. "And I suppose you know Whitney was driving down to Cheyenne this afternoon."

Brant looked puzzled. "Who's Whitney? Do I know a Whitney?"

"She's the manager of that new coffee shop, Rangeland Roasters and she's the woman Ty…used to date." Rosie turned her attention to him. "I know you two aren't speaking, but if you still have her number, would you—"

"I was planning to call her after I unloaded my stuff."

"Let me help." Brant relieved him of the duffel and the bag of presents.

"Go into the rec room," Rosie said. "Nobody else is here yet."

"Thanks." He unbuttoned his sheepskin coat as he walked through the kitchen and into the rec room. As usual, the pool table had been covered with a tablecloth and chairs were grouped around it in preparation for serving the Christmas Eve meal.

Telling himself that Whitney was fine, that she had to be fine, he pulled out his phone. But as he listened to hers ring, his chest tightened and his pulse rate shot up. When the call went to voice mail he swore. Then he took a quick breath and left a message. "Hey, it's me. Call when you get this."

After he disconnected he stood in the rec room, his eyes closed and his hands shaking. He couldn't go back in the living room like that. She was probably fine. It was Christmas Eve. She might have turned off her phone so she could have uninterrupted time with her family.

All logical, but logic wasn't working for him. What if she'd ended up in that crash? What if she was hurt, scared, cold or…no, he couldn't even think about that or he'd lose it.

When his phone rang and her name popped up on the screen, the adrenaline rush was so strong he almost fumbled the call. "Whitney? Are you okay?"

She sounded hoarse. "I'm fine."

She didn't sound fine, but at least she sounded alive. "Have you been crying?"

"No, I have a cold. Why did you call?"

"Mom was worried. There was a big pileup near Casper and she asked me to make sure you weren't in it." He was such a damned coward. Couldn't even admit he'd been in total panic mode.

"Yeah, I heard about that. I went through there before it happened." She coughed. "Fortunately I was already here when it hit the news."

"Good. So your parents didn't have to worry."

"No. Sorry Rosie did, though." She coughed again. "Please tell her Merry Christmas for me. Herb, too, and anybody else who's there."

"I will. I'm sorry you're sick."

"Yeah, well, stuff happens, as they say. You'd better go report back to Rosie that I'm fine so she can stop worrying."

"Right."

"Listen, I need to go. They put *The Grinch* on pause so I could call you back. I don't want to keep them waiting."

"Okay."

"'Bye."

"Whitney, wait."

"What?"

"Rosie was worried, but I… I was scared shitless. I had planned to call even before she asked me to. When you didn't answer…" He blew out a breath. "I'm really glad you weren't in that pileup."

"Me, too." She hesitated. "Merry Christmas, Ty." And she disconnected.

He should have wished her a Merry Christmas, too,

damn it. Taking a long, slow breath, he walked back into the living room to deliver the news.

TY DID HIS BEST to take part in the evening's festivities. Lexi and Cade were at her parents' house for Christmas Eve dinner, but Damon and Phil came to the ranch and brought Phil's dad and her stepmother. Ty remembered hearing that Phil's mom had died when she was little, and a few years ago her dad had finally remarried.

At the time Ty had learned about Phil's mom he'd thought she was lucky because she'd been spared the intense grief of losing a mother she'd known for years. His thinking must be changing. When he looked at her now, he felt sorry that she'd never known her mother at all. Sure, she had her dad, but that wasn't the same as having memories of both parents.

He'd been blessed with a terrific mother and father, even if he'd only had them the first fourteen years of his life. Then he'd been gifted with Rosie and Herb, and Rosie was a lot more maternal than Phil's new stepmom. Maybe, just maybe, he was beginning to feel a little less sorry for himself.

Fortunately he didn't have to make conversation during the meal. He appreciated that because he had some thinking to do about Whitney Jones.

Then Brant surprised them all with the news that he'd left his steady job at the ranch in Cody. He'd discovered that his talent for starting foals was in demand, and he'd decided to freelance. Ty paid more attention to that discussion.

He could picture his buddy becoming very successful. Brant's sense of humor and calm acceptance of whatever came his way had a soothing effect on both mares and foals. Hell, Brant had a soothing effect on him.

In the first weeks of living at the ranch, Ty had been enraged by Brant's unflappable nature. For Ty, who'd been spoiling for a fight, Brant had been a challenge because the guy wouldn't respond to his taunts. Eventually Brant had invited him to throw a punch, and another and another.

Ty had laid into him and Brant had stood there taking it until Ty had worn himself out. Finally he'd realized that this huge guy who could have flattened him at any time wasn't going to fight back. Humbled, he'd apologized for being a total asshole. They'd been close friends ever since.

After the evening wound down, Ty picked up his duffel, put on his coat and hat, and walked with Brant through the cold night to their cabin. Brant had been down earlier to turn on some lights and the baseboard heater. The place was nice and warm by the time they walked in.

It was late, so they quickly got ready for bed. The guys used to squabble about who got the top bunk, but the new loft beds gave everyone a top bunk. Brant had already claimed one on the left and Ty took the right side.

He settled down in the darkness as the familiar scent of wood and the whirr of the heater reminded him of when he'd lived at the ranch. "I think it's great that you're going to freelance," he said.

Brant didn't answer right away.

Ty decided he might be asleep, so he propped his hands behind his head. He had more thinking to do.

"Thanks," Brant said.

"So you are awake."

"Nope. I talk in my sleep now. It's my new thing."

Ty laughed. "Should be an interesting night. What kinds of things do you talk about?"

"Tonight I'll probably talk about Tyrone Slater."

"Oh, really?"

"I'll speculate on why he was off in la-la land all through dinner."

"I was hoping nobody noticed."

"They probably didn't, what with deciding on cake flavors and bridesmaid dresses and music selections."

How like Brant to say something like that so he wouldn't feel bad. "But you noticed."

"I know Tyrone pretty damned well. Being quiet isn't his usual setting."

"I was thinking about Whitney."

"I'm not surprised." Brant's tone became more serious, although with Brant serious didn't usually last long. "When I mentioned the pileup you got all twitchy. I didn't understand why until I heard about your ex being on that road."

"I'm in love with her." It was such a relief to say it.

"I figured that."

"She's in love with me, too." That sounded really stupid. They loved each other and yet on Christmas Eve he was in one place and she was in another. "But I'm not the right guy for her."

"You'd know that better than me."

"She needs someone who can open up about his childhood. I'm not." Oh, wasn't he special? She'd had one request and he couldn't manage it because he was too sensitive. Sheesh.

"That's your prerogative, bro. You don't have to spill your guts to anyone."

"I know, but…"

"Hey, someone else will come along."

"Not like her."

"Maybe even better than her! Life's full of surprises. Lots of fish in the sea. You never know."

"Yes, I do, damn it. You can't know because you've never met her, but she's the best thing that ever happened to me and I was insane to let her go. She's right about my parents, too. I need to talk about them. They were great. They deserve for people to know that. She deserves to know them."

"Just so you're sure," Brant said. "It's a big step."

"I'm sure. I'm driving down there tomorrow."

"Okay. Do you know where her parents live?"

"No."

"What's their last name?"

"Jones."

"Oh, that's helpful."

"But I know their first names, Art and Ellen. I'll look online. I'll find them."

"Or you could play it cool and wait until she comes back up here. If she's running that coffee shop she can't stay in Cheyenne forever."

"I don't want to play it cool. It has to be tomorrow."

"Personally I'd wait until she's back in town. A lot less trouble."

"That won't work for me. I need to wish her Merry Christmas."

TRAFFIC HAD BEEN fairly heavy on Christmas Eve, but not many people were on the road Christmas Day. The ice had melted off the pavement and nothing remained of the big pileup except a twisted bumper on the shoulder. Ty made good time.

He wished he had a present for her, but he hadn't decided on one before the breakup and afterward he'd abandoned the idea. Showing up on Christmas Day without a present seemed wrong, but some doodad from a truck stop didn't shout *I love you*.

She might not want to hear it after all he'd put her through. He clung to what she'd told him before he'd become the ass who walked out on her. She'd said if he ever changed his mind, he'd know where to find her.

But he didn't know where to find her folks, and the search had taken a little longer than he'd anticipated. He'd had to pay money to a site that finally gave him the address. While part of him was horrified at the availability of personal information for a fee, the other part of him was incredibly grateful.

The house was a modest two-story, not all that different from the one he'd grown up in. The walk had been shoveled and he could smell woodsmoke. Lights lined the porch roof although they weren't on now, and twin wreaths of fragrant evergreen boughs hung on either side of the storm door. He thought that might be significant.

Art answered the door wearing a red sweat suit that looked like it might be a Christmas present, and Christmas music played in the background. He blinked when he saw Ty. "Uh, hi. Merry Christmas."

"Merry Christmas to you." Crashing their private family celebration might not win him points but Whitney was in this cozy house and he needed her desperately.

"Who is it, Art?"

Ty recognized Ellen's voice.

"It's Whitney's boyfriend." He paused in confusion. "Or the one who used to be her boyfriend."

"Well, invite him in, for heaven's sake. I'll get Whitney."

Art opened the storm door and stepped back. "Come on in. We have eggnog. Do you like eggnog?"

"I like whatever you're serving."

"That's a great attitude." Art beamed at him. "Been watching the games?"

"A little. Work's been intense." Ty hadn't given the football season another thought after leaving Whitney's apartment the day they'd said goodbye. Or rather, he'd said goodbye. She hadn't wanted to.

"Both our teams are still in the hunt!"

"Great!"

"Let me take your coat and hat."

"Thanks." Ty handed them over and glanced around at a scene right out of a greeting card commercial. A wood fire blazed in the brick fireplace and a sturdy spruce full of homemade ornaments sat in a corner with its lights on and the opened gifts lovingly placed around it.

The aroma of roasting turkey hung in the air. Photo albums lay open on the coffee table and crocheted throws were draped over the sofa as if someone had recently abandoned them. Like Whitney.

He walked over to the mantel to look at a picture of two identical teenaged girls, but he recognized Whitney immediately. Both the tilt of her chin and the sparkle in her eyes were imprinted on his heart.

"Me and Selena."

He turned to face her as she walked into the room wearing a light blue sweat suit that also looked like a Christmas present. Ellen must enjoy giving sweat suits. But Whitney's parents had mysteriously disappeared. "You're the one on the right."

"Yes." Her eyes were puffy and her nose was red, but she was still the most beautiful woman in the world.

"I love you." He hadn't meant to blurt it out like that.

Her eyes widened. "I love you, too, but what difference does that make?"

"As it turns out, it makes all the difference." He moved toward her.

She edged away. "I don't want you to catch this. It's nasty."

"I won't catch it." He kept moving. "And even if I did, I wouldn't give a damn. I love you. We're going to share all kinds of things over the years—germs, memories, heartache—the works."

"Are you sure?" She looked like a kid who couldn't believe the new pony was actually hers. "I wasn't kidding before. I want it all."

Her hesitation tore at his heart but he couldn't blame her for doubting. He'd been pretty damned stubborn. "That's what I'm offering," he said softly. "You'll get it all, the whole shebang." He gestured toward the photo albums lying open on the coffee table. "Including things like that."

"We go through them every Christmas."

"Great idea."

"You really think so?"

"Yes, ma'am. On my way here I stopped at my apartment and grabbed the sealed box. It's out in the truck. I want you to be there when I open it."

She sniffed. "Oh, Ty."

He started toward her again.

She waved him away. "Really, stay back. I'm a mess."

"I don't care. I want to hold you. Please."

She hesitated.

"Please."

"I guess holding's okay. Kissing's out of the question, though. I can't breathe, let alone kiss."

"No worries." He gathered her close and suddenly his world made sense again. "I remember what your kiss feels like so I can use my imagination." He looked into her eyes. "Memories are so precious."

"Yes, they are." Her gaze filled with the love he'd seen there the day he'd left, the love he'd almost thrown away.

"I want to share my life with you, Whitney. All of it—the old and the new. Will you have me?"

"I think we established weeks ago that I will." She slipped her arms around his neck. "But just to be clear, are we promising to love, honor and cherish?"

"God, I hope so."

"Then I'm in."

His life clicked into focus. Whitney wanted to be with him forever. A guy didn't get any luckier than that. But there were still issues. "I don't know what we'll do about the long commute."

She smiled. "Maybe all we have to do is commit to loving each other and the rest will work itself out."

"You know, I have a feeling it will."

"Me, too." She cradled his face in both hands. "We might be able to manage one little kiss. Just make it quick."

He tried to make it quick, but once his lips found hers, he didn't want to leave.

Eventually she pulled away, gasping and coughing.

He waited until she'd blown her nose and her eyes stopped watering. "I guarantee that's a memory we'll cherish, me trying to kiss you after proposing and nearly asphyxiating you in the process."

She smiled at him. "Yep. The first of many."

"So many." But he took a mental picture of this one, when Whitney Jones, with a red nose, chapped lips and watering eyes, agreed to spend a lifetime with him. It would be his favorite memory of all.

Epilogue

January, Thunder Mountain Ranch

ROSIE PACED IN the kitchen waiting impatiently for Brant to answer his phone. She'd held off until evening to call him in hopes he wouldn't be busy training a foal, but he could be tending to a pregnant mare about to give birth. That kind of thing didn't happen on a nine-to-five schedule.

"Hi, Mom." His deep voice always sounded slightly amused. He was a man who laughed easily. His sunny disposition had amazed her from the start, considering where he'd come from.

"Brant, I'm so glad I caught you. Can you talk?"

"Been doing it since I was about two and so far, so good."

"Oh, for pity's sake." But she laughed because that sort of comeback was so him. "I wanted to tell you the big news. Whitney called today and she's moving back to Cheyenne."

"That's cool, but Ty said she loves managing that new coffee shop."

"She does, but she'll also love managing the old one

in Cheyenne. Her boss Ginny has a hankering to live up here and wants to swap with her. Ty and Whitney are house hunting and I predict they'll set a wedding date soon."

"That's terrific. Ol' Tyrone really loves that woman. I've never seen him so twirly about someone."

"Thank goodness he is. He gave me a scare when he broke up with her. But that isn't the main reason I called. Looks like we're going to board a pregnant mare and incorporate the foal's birth into the first summer session in June."

"Excellent. The kids will love that."

"They will! We put a notice in our online newsletter this week and the last four spots were snapped up."

"Glad to hear that, Mom."

"It's so exciting. Herb will handle the actual birth, of course, but as you might have already guessed, I want to hire you to demonstrate the proper training of a new foal. Do you have time?"

He chuckled. "Let me check my busy schedule."

"I know you're probably in demand, but I—"

"I'm kidding! Of course I'll do it. I just started the freelance business so I'm not booked up yet. But even if I had been, I'd figure out a way to help. You got a due date?"

"Should be around the second week of June, but I'd like to have you here by June first in case she's early. We can always find something for you to do. We'll have sixteen teenagers on the premises, so there'll be plenty of work to go around."

"Sounds like fun."

"It will be! And thank you so much. I was hoping you'd say yes, especially after I told Aria you'd be perfect."

"She's the mare's owner?"

"Yes, and she has a special purpose for this foal so having you start it will thrill her to death."

"What sort of purpose?"

"A riding accident put her brother in a wheelchair and he's understandably depressed. She's hoping this foal will inspire him to work harder to get out of that chair."

"That's a big job for a little horse."

"I know, but I think it could work. I watched you boys respond to our horses. I saw some miracles take place here."

"You're the miracle, Mom. You and Dad."

The unexpected compliment made her tear up. "What a lovely thing to say."

"Glad you like it. I saw it on a greeting card."

"Oh, *you*." That was so Brant. Couldn't ever stay serious for long. "All right, then. We're all set. Love you, son."

"Love you, too, Mom."

After she disconnected the call she held the phone to her heart as if to keep him with her a little longer. Good thing those teenagers would start arriving in June. She missed her boys.

* * * * *

If you like fun, sexy and steamy stories with strong heroines and irresistible heroes, you'll love THE HARDER YOU FALL *by* New York Times *bestselling author Gena Showalter—featuring Jessie Kay Dillon and Lincoln West, the sexy bachelor who's breaking all his rules for this rowdy Southern belle...*

Turn the page for a sneak peek at THE HARDER YOU FALL!

West had brought a date.

The realization hit Jessie Kay like a bolt of lightning in a freak storm. Great! Wonderful! While she'd opted not to bring Daniel, and thus make West the only single person present—and embarrassingly alone—he'd chosen his next two-month "relationship" and hung Jessie Kay out to dry.

Hidden in the back of the sanctuary, Jessie Kay stood in the doorway used by church personnel and scowled. Harlow had asked for—cough, banshee-screeched, cough—a status report. Jessie Kay had abandoned her precious curling iron in order to sneak a peek at the guys.

Now she pulled her phone out of the pocket in her dress to text Daniel. Oops. She'd missed a text.

Sunny: Party 2nite?????

She made a mental note to respond to Sunny later and drafted her note to Daniel.

I'm at the church. How fast can you get here? I need a friend/date for Harlow's wedding

A response didn't come right away. She knew he'd gone on a date last night and the girl had stayed the night with him. How did she know? Because he'd texted Jessie Kay to ask how early he could give the snoring girl the boot.

Sooo glad I never hooked up with him.

Finally, a vibration signaled a response.

Any other time I'd race to your rescue, even though weddings are snorefests. Today I'm in the city on a job

He'd started some kind of high-risk security firm with a few of his Army buddies.

Her: Fine. You suck. I clearly need to rethink our friendship

Daniel: I'll make it up to you, swear. Want to have dinner later???

She slid her phone back in place without responding, adding his name to her mental note. If he wasn't going to ignore his responsibilities whenever she had a minor need, he deserved to suffer for a little while.

Of its own accord, Jessie Kay's gaze returned to West. The past week, she'd seen him only twice. Both times, she'd gone to the farmhouse to help her sister with sandwiches and casseroles, and he'd taken one look at her, grabbed his keys and driven off.

Would it have killed him to acknowledge her presence by calling her by some hateful name, per usual? After all, he'd had the nerve to flirt with her at the diner, to look at her as if she'd stripped naked and begged him to have *her* for dessert. And now he ignored her? Men! This one in particular.

Her irritation grew as he introduced his date to Kenna Starr and her fiancé, Dane Michaelson. Kenna was a stunning redhead who'd always been Brook Lynn's partner in crime. The girl who'd done what Jessie Kay had not, saving her sister every time she'd gotten into trouble.

Next up was an introduction to Daphne Roberts, the mother of Jase's nine-year-old daughter, Hope, then Brad Lintz, Daphne's boyfriend.

Jase and Beck joined the happy group, but the brunette never looked away from West, as if he was speaking the good Lord's gospel. Her adoration was palpable.

A sharp pang had Jessie Kay clutching her chest. *Too young for a heart attack.*

Indigestion?

Yeah. Had to be.

The couple should have looked odd together. West was too tall and the brunette was far too short for him. A skyscraper next to a one-story house. But somehow, despite their height difference, the two actually complemented each other.

And really, the girl's adoration had to be good for West, buoying him the way Daniel's praise often buoyed Jessie Kay. Only on a much higher level, considering the girl was more than a friend to West.

Deep down, Jessie Kay was actually…happy for West. As crappy as his childhood had been, he deserved a nice slice of contentment.

Look at me, acting like a big girl and crap.

When West wrapped his arm around the brunette's waist, drawing her closer, Jessie Kay's nails dug into her palms.

I'm happy for him, remember? Besides, big girls

didn't want to push other women in front of a speeding bus.

Jessie Kay's phone buzzed. Another text. This one from Brook Lynn.

Hurry! Bridezilla is on a rampage!!!

Her: Tell her the guys look amazing in their tuxes—no stains or tears yet—and the room is gorgeous. Or just tell her NOTHING HAS FREAKING CHANGED

The foster bros had gone all out even though the ceremony was to be a small and intimate affair. There were red and white roses at the corner of every pew, and in front of the pulpit was an ivory arch with wispy jewel-encrusted lace.

With a sigh, she added an adorable smiley face to her message, because it was cute and it said I'm not yelling at you. My temper is not engaged.

Send.

Brook Lynn: Harlow wants a play-by-play of the action

Fine.

Beck is now speaking w/Pastor Washington. Jase, Dane, Kenna, Daphne & Brad are engaged in conversation, while Hope is playing w/ her doll on the floor. Happy?

She didn't add that West was focused on the stunning brunette, who was still clinging to his side.

The girl…she had a familiar face—*where have I seen her?*—and a body so finely honed Jessie Kay wanted to stuff a few thousand Twinkies down her throat just to make it fair for the rest of the female population. Her designer dress was made of ebony silk and hugged her curves like a besotted lover.

Like West would be doing tonight?

Grinding her teeth, Jessie Kay slid her gaze over her own gown. One she'd sewn in her spare time. Not bad—actually kind of awesome—but compared to Great Bod's delicious apple it was a rotten orange.

A wave of jealousy swept over her. Dang it! Jealousy was stupid. Jessie Kay was no can of dog food in the looks department. In fact, she was well able to hold her own against anyone, anywhere, anytime. But…but…

A lot of baggage came with her.

West suddenly stiffened, as if he knew he was being watched. He turned. Her heart slamming against her ribs with enough force to break free and escape, she darted into Harlow's bridal chamber—the choir room.

Harlow finished curling her thick mass of hair as Brook Lynn gave her lips a final swipe of gloss.

"Welcome to my nightmare," Jessie Kay announced. "I might as well put in rollers, pull on a pair of mom jeans and buy ten thousand cats." Cats! Want! "I'm officially an old maid without any decent prospects."

Brook Lynn wrinkled her brow. "What are you talking about?"

"Everyone is here, including West and his date. I'm the only single person in our group, which means you guys have to set me up with your favorite guy friends. Obviously I'm looking for a nine or ten. Make it happen. Please and thank you."

Harlow went still. "West brought a date? Who is it?"

Had a curl of steam just risen from her nostrils? "Just some girl."

Harlow pressed her hands against a stomach that had to be dancing with nerves. "I don't want *just some girl* at my first wedding."

"You planning your divorce to Beck already?"

Harlow scowled at her. "Not funny. You know we're planning a larger ceremony next year."

Jessie Kay raised her hands, palms out. "You're right, you're right. And you totally convinced me. I'll kick the bitch out pronto." *And I'll love every second of it—on Harlow's behalf.*

"No. No. I don't want a scene." Stomping her foot, Harlow added, "What was West thinking? He's ruined *everything.*"

Ooo-kay. A wee bit dramatic, maybe. "I doubt he was thinking at all. If that boy ever had an idea, it surely died of loneliness." Too much? "Anyway. I'm sure you could use a glass or six of champagne. I'll open the bottle for us—for you. You're welcome."

A wrist corsage hit her square in the chest.

"This is *my* day, Jessica Dillon." Harlow thumped her chest. "Mine! You will remain stone-cold sober, or I will remove your head, place it on a stick and wave it around while your sister sobs over your bleeding corpse."

Wow. "That's pretty specific, but I feel you. No alcohol for me, ma'am." She gave a jaunty salute. "I mean, no alcohol for me, Miss Bridezilla, sir."

"Ha-ha." Harlow morphed from fire-breathing dragon to fairy-tale princess in an instant, twirling in a circle. "Now stop messing around and tell me how amazing I look. And don't hesitate to use words like *exquisite* and *magical.*"

The hair at her temples had been pulled back, but the rest hung to her elbows in waves so dark they glimmered blue in the light. The gown had capped sleeves and a straight bustline with a cinched-in waist and pleats that flowed all the way to the floor, covering the sensible flats she'd chosen based on West's advice. "You look… exquisitely magical."

"Magically exquisite," Brook Lynn said with a nod.

"My scars aren't hideous?" Self-conscious, Harlow smoothed a hand over the multitude of jagged pink lines running between her breasts, courtesy of an attack she'd miraculously survived as a teenage girl.

"Are you kidding? Those scars make you look bad-ass." Jessie Kay curled a few more pieces of hair, adding, "I'm bummed my skin is so flawless."

Harlow snorted. "Yes, let's shed a tear for you."

Jessie Kay gave her sister the stink eye. "You better not be like this for your wedding. I won't survive two of you."

Brook Lynn held up her well-manicured hands, all innocence.

"Well." She glanced at a wristwatch she wasn't wearing, doing her best impression of West. "We've got twenty minutes before the festivities kick off. Need anything?"

Harlow's hands returned to her stomach, the color draining from her cheeks in a hurry. "Yes. Beck."

Blinking, certain she'd misheard, she fired off a quick "Excuse me?" Heck. Deck. Neck. Certainly not Beck. "Grooms aren't supposed to see—"

"I need Beck." Harlow stomped her foot. *"Now."*

"Have you changed your mind?" Brook Lynn asked. "If so, we'll—"

"No, no. Nothing like that." Harlow launched into a quick pace, marching back and forth through the room.

"I just… I need to see him. He hates change, and this is the biggest one of all, and I need to talk to him before I totally. Flip. Out. Okay? All right?"

"This isn't that big a change, honey. Not really." Who would have guessed Jessie Kay would be a voice of reason in a situation like this. Or *any* situation? "You guys live together already."

"Beck!" she insisted. "Beck, Beck, Beck."

"Temper tantrums are not attractive." Jessie Kay shared a concerned look with her sister, who nodded. "All right. One Beck coming up." As fast as her heels would allow, she made her way back to the sanctuary.

She purposely avoided West's general direction, focusing only on the groom. "Harlow has decided to throw millions of years' worth of tradition out the window. She wants to see you without delay. Are you wearing a cup? I'd wear a cup. Good luck."

He'd been in the middle of a conversation with Jase, and like Harlow, he quickly paled. "Is something wrong with her?" He didn't stick around for an answer, rushing past Jessie Kay without actually judging the distance between them, almost knocking her over.

As she stumbled, West flew over and latched on to her wrist to help steady her. The contact nearly buckled her knees. His hands were calloused, his fingers firm. His strength unparalleled and his skin hot enough to burn. Electric tingles rushed through her, the world around her fading from existence until they were the only two people in existence.

Fighting for every breath, she stared up at him. His gaze dropped to her lips and narrowed, his focus savagely carnal and primal in its possessiveness, as if he saw nothing else, either—wanted nothing and no one else ever. But as he slowly lowered his arm and stepped away from her, the world snapped back into motion.

The bastard brought a date.

Right. She cleared her throat, embarrassed by the force of her reaction to him. "Thanks."

A muscle jumped in his jaw. A sign of anger? "May I speak with you privately?"

Uh… "Why?"

"Please."

What the what now? Had Lincoln West actually said the word *please* to her? *Her?* "Whatever you have to say to me—" an insult, no doubt "—can wait. You should return to your flavor of the year." Opting for honesty, she grudgingly added, "You guys look good together."

The muscle jumped again, harder, faster. "You think we look good together?"

"Very much so." Two perfect people. "I'm not being sarcastic, if that's what you're getting at. Who is she?"

"Monica Gentry. Fitness guru based in the city."

Well. That explained the sense of familiarity. And the body. Jessie Kay had once briefly considered thinking about exercising along with Monica's video. Then she'd found a bag of KIT KAT Minis and the insane idea went back to hell, where it belonged. "She's a good choice for you. Beautiful. Successful. Driven. And despite what you think about me, despite the animosity between us, I want you happy."

And not just because of his crappy childhood, she realized. He was a part of her family, for better or worse. A girl made exceptions for family. Even the douche bags.

His eyes narrowed to tiny slits. "We're going to speak privately, Jessie Kay, whether you agree or not. The only decision you need to make is whether or not you'll walk. I'm more than willing to carry you."

A girl also had the right to smack family. "You're just going to tell me to change my hideous dress, and I'm going to tell you I'm fixing to cancel your birth certificate."

When Harlow had proclaimed *Wear whatever you want*, Jessie Kay had done just that, creating a bloodred, off-the-shoulder, pencil-skirt dress that molded to her curves like a second skin...made from leftover material for drapes.

Scarlett O'Hara has nothing on me!

Jessie Kay was proud of her work, but she wasn't blind to its flaws. Knotted threads in the seams. Years had passed since she'd sewn anything, and her skills were rusty.

West gave her another once—twice—over as fire smoldered in his eyes. "Why would I tell you to change?" His voice dipped, nothing but smoke and gravel. "You and that dress are a fantasy come true."

Uh, what the what now? Had Lincoln West just called her *a fantasy*?

Almost can't process...

"Maybe you should take me to the ER, West. I think I just had a brain aneurysm." She rubbed her temples. "I'm hallucinating."

"Such a funny girl." He ran his tongue over his teeth, snatched her hand and while Monica called his name, dragged Jessie Kay to a small room in back. A cleaning closet, the air sharp with antiseptic. What little space was available was consumed by overstuffed shelves.

"When did you decide to switch careers and become a caveman?" she asked.

"When you decided to switch careers and become a femme fatale."

Have mercy on my soul.

He released her to run his fingers through his hair, leaving the strands in sexy spikes around his head. "Listen. I owe you an apology for the way I've treated you in the past. The way I've acted today. I shouldn't have manhandled you, and I'm very sorry."

Her eyes widened. Seriously, what the heck had happened to this man? In five minutes, he'd upended everything she'd come to expect from him.

And he wasn't done! "I'm sorry for every hurtful thing I've ever said to you. I'm sorry for making you feel bad about who you are and what you've done. I'm sorry—"

"Stop. Just stop." She placed her hands over her ears in case he failed to heed her order. "I don't understand what's happening."

He gently removed her hands and held on tight to her wrists. "What's happening? I'm owning my mistakes and hoping you're in a forgiving mood."

"You want to be my friend?" The words squeaked from her.

"I...do."

Why the hesitation? "Here's the problem. You're a dog and I'm a cat, and we're never going to get along."

One corner of his mouth quirked with lazy amusement, causing a flutter to skitter through her pulse. "I think you're wrong...kitten."

Kitten. A freakishly adorable nickname, and absolutely perfect for her. But also absolutely unexpected.

Oh, she'd known he'd give her one sooner or later. He and his friends enjoyed renaming the women in their lives. Jase always called Brook Lynn "angel" and Beck called Harlow everything from "beauty" to "hag," her initials. Well, HAG prewedding. But Jessie Kay had prepared herself for "demoness" or the always classic "bitch."

"Dogs and cats can be friends," he said, "especially when the dog minds his manners. I promise you, things will be different from now on."

"Well." Reeling, she could come up with no witty reply. "We could try, I guess."

"Good." His gaze dropped to her lips, heated a few more degrees. "Now all we have to do is decide what kind of friends we should be."

Her heart started kicking up a fuss all over again, breath abandoning her lungs. "What do you mean?"

"Text frequently? Call each other occasionally? Only speak when we're with our other friends?" He backed her into a shelf and cans rattled, threatening to fall. "Or should we be friends with benefits?"

The tingles returned, sweeping over her skin and sinking deep, deep into bone. Her entire body ached with sudden need and it was so powerful it nearly felled her. How long since a man had focused the full scope of his masculinity on her? Too long and never like this. Somehow West had reduced her to a quivering mess of femininity and whoremones.

"I vote…we only speak when we're with our other friends," she said, embarrassed by the breathless tremor in her voice.

"What if I want all of it?" He placed his hands at her temples and several of the cans rolled to the floor. "The texts, the calls…and the benefits."

"No?" A question? Really? "No to the last. You have a date."

He scowled at her as if *she'd* done something wrong. "See, that's the real problem, kitten. I don't want her. I want you."

WEST CALLED HIMSELF a thousand kinds of fool. He'd planned to apologize, return to the sanctuary, witness his friend's wedding and start the countdown with Monica. The moment he'd gotten Jessie Kay inside the closet, her pecans-and-cinnamon scent in his nose, those plans burned to ash. Only one thing mattered.

Getting his hands on her.

From day one, she'd been a vertical g-force too strong to deny, pulling, pulling, *pulling* him into a bottomless vortex. He'd fought it every minute of every day since meeting her, and he'd gotten nowhere fast. Why not give in? Stop the madness?

Just once...

"We've been dancing around this for months," he said. "I'm scum for picking here and now to hash this out with you, and I'll care tomorrow. Right now, I think it's time we did something about our feelings."

"I don't..." She began to soften against him, only to snap to attention. "No. Absolutely not. I can't."

"You *won't.*" *But I can change your mind...*

She nibbled on her bottom lip.

Something he would kill to do. So he did it. He leaned into her, caught her bottom lip between his teeth and ran the plump morsel through. "Do you want me, Jessie Kay?"

Her eyes closed for a moment, a shiver rocking her. "You say you'll care tomorrow, so I'll give you an answer then. As for today, I… I… I'm leaving." But she made no effort to move away, and he knew. She did want him. As badly as he wanted her. "Yes. Leaving. Any moment now…"

Acting without thought—purely on instinct—he placed his hands on her waist and pressed her against the hard line of his body. "I want you to stay. I want you, period."

"West." The new tremor in her voice injected his every masculine instinct with adrenaline, jacking him up. "You said it yourself. You're scum. This is wrong."

Anticipation raced denial to the tip of his tongue, and won by a photo finish. "Do you care?" He caressed his way to her ass and cupped the perfect globes, then urged her forward to rub her against the long length of his erection. The woman who'd tormented his days and invaded his dreams moaned a decadent sound of satisfaction and it did something to him. Made his need for her *worse*.

She wasn't what he should want, but somehow she'd become everything he could not resist, and he was tired, so damn tired, of walking, hell, running away from her.

"Do you?" he insisted. "Say yes, and *I'll* be the one to leave. I don't want you to regret this." He wanted her desperate for more.

She looked away from him, licked her lips. "Right at this moment? No. I don't care." As soft as a whisper.

Triumph filled him, his clasp on her tightening.

"But tomorrow…" she added.

Yes. Tomorrow. He wasn't the only one who'd been running from the sizzle between them, but today, with her admission ringing in his ears, he wasn't letting her get away. One look at her, that's all it had taken to ruin his plans. Now she would pay the price. Now she would make everything better.

"I *will* regret it," she said. "This is a mistake I've made too many times in the past."

Different emotions played over her features. Features so delicate he was consumed by the need to protect her from anything and anyone...but himself.

He saw misery, desire, fear, regret, hope and anger. The anger concerned him. This Southern belle could knock a man's testicles into his throat with a single swipe of her knee. Even still, West didn't walk away.

"For all we know, the world will end tomorrow. Let's focus on today. You tell me what you want me to do," he said, nuzzling his nose against her cheek, "and I'll do it."

More tremors rocked her. She traced her delicate hands up his tie and gave the knot a little shake, an action that was sexy, sweet and wicked all at once. "I want you...to go back to your date. You and I, we'll be friends as agreed, and we'll pretend this never happened." She pushed him, but he didn't budge.

His date. Yeah, he'd forgotten about Monica before Jessie Kay had mentioned her a few minutes ago. But then, he'd gotten used to forgetting everything whenever the luscious blonde entered a room. Everything about her consumed every part of him, and it was more than irritating, it was a sickness to be cured, an obstacle to be overcome and an addiction to be avoided. If they did this, he would suffer from his own regrets, but there was no question he would love the ride.

He bunched up the hem of her skirt, his fingers brushing the silken heat of her bare thigh. Her breath hitched, driving him wild. "You've told me what you *think* you should want me to do." He rasped the words against her mouth, hovering over her, not touching her but teasing with what could be. "Now tell me what you really want me to do."

Navy blues peered up at him, beseeching; the fight drained out of her, leaving only need and raw vulnerability. "I'm only using you for sex—said no guy ever. But that's what you're going to do. Isn't it? You're going to use me and lose me, just like the others."

Her features were utterly *ravaged*, and in that moment, he hated himself. Because she was right. Whether he took her for a single night or every night for two months, the end result would be the same. No matter how much it hurt her—no matter how much it hurt *him*—he would walk away.

COMING NEXT MONTH FROM

HARLEQUIN® Blaze®

Available December 15, 2015

#875 PLEASING HER SEAL
Uniformly Hot!
by Anne Marsh
Wedding blogger Madeline Holmes lives and breathes romance—
from the sidelines. That is, until Navy SEAL Mason Black promises
to fulfill all of her fantasies at an exclusive island resort. But is
Mason her ultimate fantasy—could he be "the one"?

#876 RED HOT
Hotshot Heroes
by Lisa Childs
Forest ranger firefighter Wyatt Andrews battles the flames
to keep others safe, but who will protect *him* from the fiery
redhead who thinks he's endangering her little brother?

#877 HER SEXY VEGAS COWBOY
by Ali Olson
Jessica Gainey decides to take a wild ride with rancher
Aaron Weathers while she's in Vegas. But when it's time to
go home, how can she put those hot nights—and her sexy
cowboy—behind her?

#878 PLAYING TO WIN
by Taryn Leigh Taylor
Reporter Holly Evans is determined to uncover star hockey
captain Luke Maguire's sinful secrets. But when *he's* the one
who turns the heat up on *her*, their sexy game is on...

**YOU CAN FIND MORE INFORMATION ON UPCOMING HARLEQUIN® TITLES,
FREE EXCERPTS AND MORE AT WWW.HARLEQUIN.COM.**

HBCNM1215

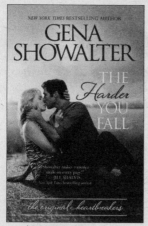

SPECIAL EXCERPT FROM

When Maddie Holmes first meets Mason Black she has
no idea he's a Navy SEAL on an undercover mission...
but she's about to find out all his secrets!

Read on for a sneak preview of
PLEASING HER SEAL by **Anne Marsh**
part of Harlequin Blaze's
UNIFORMLY HOT! miniseries.

Fantasy Island advertised itself as an idyllic slice of
paradise located on the Caribbean Sea—the perfect place
for a destination wedding or honeymoon. The elegant type
on the resort brochure promised barefoot luxury, discreet
hedonism and complete wish fulfillment. Maddie's job
was to translate those naughty promises into sexy web
copy that would drive traffic to her blog and fill her bank
account with much-needed advertising dollars.

The summit beckoned, and she stepped out into a
small clearing overlooking the ocean.

"Good view?" At the sound of the deep male voice
behind her, Maddie flinched, arms and legs jerking
in shock. Her camera flew forward as she scrambled
backward.

Strong male fingers fastened around her wrist. Panicked, she grabbed her croissant and lobbed it at the guy,
followed by her coffee. He cursed and dodged.

"It's not a good day to jump without a chute." He
tugged her away from the edge of the lookout, and she
got her first good look at him. Not a stranger. *Okay, then*.

Her heart banged hard against her rib cage, pummeling her lungs, before settling back into a more normal rhythm. *Mason.* Mason I-Can't-Be-Bothered-To-Tell-You-My-Last-Name-But-I'm-A-Stud. He led the cooking classes by the pool. She'd written him off as good-looking but aloof, not certain if she'd spotted a spark of potential interest in his dark eyes. Wishful thinking or dating potential—it was probably a moot point now, since she'd just pegged him with her mocha.

He didn't seem pissed off. On the contrary, he simply rocked back on his haunches, hands held out in front of him. *I come in peace,* she thought, fortunately too out of breath to giggle. The side of his shirt sported a dark stain from her coffee. Oh, goody. She'd actually scalded him. Way to make an impression on a poor, innocent guy. This was why her dating life sucked.

She tried to wheeze out an apology, but he shook his head.

"I scared you."

"You think?"

"That wasn't my intention." The look on his face was part chagrin, part repentance. Worked for her.

"I'll put a bell around your neck." Where had he learned to move so quietly?

"Why don't we start over?" He stuck out a hand. A big, masculine, slightly muddy hand. She probably shouldn't want to seize his fingers like a lifeline. "I'm Mason Black."

Don't miss PLEASING HER SEAL by Anne Marsh,
available January 2016 wherever
Harlequin® Blaze® books and ebooks are sold.

www.Harlequin.com

HBEXP1215

REQUEST YOUR FREE BOOKS!
2 FREE NOVELS PLUS 2 FREE GIFTS!

HARLEQUIN®

Blaze®

red-hot reads!

YES! Please send me 2 FREE Harlequin® Blaze® novels and my 2 FREE gifts (gifts are worth about $10). After receiving them, if I don't wish to receive any more books, I can return the shipping statement marked "cancel." If I don't cancel, I will receive 4 brand-new novels every month and be billed just $4.74 per book in the U.S. or $5.21 per book in Canada. That's a savings of at least 14% off the cover price. It's quite a bargain. Shipping and handling is just 50¢ per book in the U.S. and 75¢ per book in Canada.* I understand that accepting the 2 free books and gifts places me under no obligation to buy anything. I can always return a shipment and cancel at any time. Even if I never buy another book, the two free books and gifts are mine to keep forever.

150/350 HDN GH2D

Name _____ (PLEASE PRINT) _____

Address _____ Apt. # _____

City _____ State/Prov. _____ Zip/Postal Code _____

Signature (if under 18, a parent or guardian must sign)

Mail to the **Reader Service**:
IN U.S.A.: P.O. Box 1867, Buffalo, NY 14240-1867
IN CANADA: P.O. Box 609, Fort Erie, Ontario L2A 5X3

Want to try two free books from another line?
Call 1-800-873-8635 or visit www.ReaderService.com.

* Terms and prices subject to change without notice. Prices do not include applicable taxes. Sales tax applicable in N.Y. Canadian residents will be charged applicable taxes. Offer not valid in Quebec. This offer is limited to one order per household. Not valid for current subscribers to Harlequin Blaze books. All orders subject to credit approval. Credit or debit balances in a customer's account(s) may be offset by any other outstanding balance owed by or to the customer. Please allow 4 to 6 weeks for delivery. Offer available while quantities last.

Your Privacy—The Reader Service is committed to protecting your privacy. Our Privacy Policy is available online at www.ReaderService.com or upon request from the Reader Service.

We make a portion of our mailing list available to reputable third parties that offer products we believe may interest you. If you prefer that we not exchange your name with third parties, or if you wish to clarify or modify your communication preferences, please visit us at www.ReaderService.com/consumerchoice or write to us at Reader Service Preference Service, P.O. Box 9062, Buffalo, NY 14240-9062. Include your complete name and address.

HB15